PRAIS

THE BL

"A feast of good old-fashioned horror, with conflicted characters, a gooey monster, and plenty of blood and guts."
— **Tim Waggoner**
Bram Stoker Award Winner
& Author of *The Forever House*

"I enjoyed the well-drawn characters, people with real flaws and fears, and loved the setting around the caves of Vik, Iceland. If you like traditional horror, stories that are scary, fun and even a bit pulpy, *The Blackening* is for you!"
— **Michael Griffin**
Shirley Jackson Award Nominee
& Author of *Armageddon House*

"*The Blackening* starts with a depiction of horror and it truly pays homage to the great *H.P. Lovecraft*. *O'Connor* is a shining star in the world of horror fiction and I recommend you get on this train now before he explodes into the global sensation he deserves to be."
— **The Horror Review** by **JournalStone**

THE BLACKENING

BOOKS BY
SEÁN O'CONNOR

The Mongrel

Weeping Season

The Blackening

Keening Country

Revelations
Horror Writers for Climate Action

The Swarm

THE BLACKENING

SEÁN O'CONNOR

CADAVER
HOUSE

Grateful acknowledgement is made to Primordial
for permission to reprint an excerpt from "The Coffin Ships"
Lyrics and music by A.A Nemtheanga and Primordial © Copyright 2005

Cadaver House
Dublin, Ireland

Legal Deposit and Library Cataloguing in Publication Data.
A catalogue record for this book is available from The National Library of Ireland.

Typeset in 11pt Bookman Old Style
Interior Design by Kenneth W. Cain

ISBN: 978-1-7384567-4-1

For Samuel

"It feels like I've been here before
Here where the animals lay down to die
So we stood alone on a distant shore
Our broken spirits in rags and tatters."

— Primordial, "The Coffin Ships"

FOREWORD
by Philip Fracassi

In the middle of the 20th Century, a wonderful new craze emerged in the United States. It was called the *Drive-In Theater*. At its peak, there were more than 4,000 Drive-In Theaters across the U.S., a place where you could jump in the car, drive to what was essentially an empty parking lot, clip a metal speaker on your window, and watch some crazy movie play out on the big screen through your windshield. Hell, sometimes you'd get out and lay on the car's hood, picking up enough ambient audio from other cars to keep you tuned in to what was happening on the screen.

The best thing about Drive-In Theaters were the movies themselves. Trust me, you weren't taking your gaggle of kids, or a hot date, to the Drive-In so you could watch some great drama, or a legal thriller, or a romantic comedy. For the most part, you were parking your Buick, buying a popcorn and a soda from the snack bar, sticking that mono speaker in the window and settling in for a night of pure, unadulterated, kickass *fun*.

Typically, this came in the form of awesome genre flicks. Horror was a big draw of the Drive-In, as was science-fiction, or better yet, a combination of the two! Folks wanted to sit in their cars and watch B-movies, where scientists became bugs, or bugs became the size of buildings, or the world was invaded by aliens, or a psycho-killer in a funky mask was slicing-and-dicing young couples just trying to have some inconvenient sex.

Which brings me to Seán O'Connor.

The first book I read by O'Connor was a go-for-broke thrill ride called *Weeping Season*. I read this novel in one sitting while on vacation in Canada, and was so impressed that I immediately posted 5-star reviews and sent Seán a note via Facebook (and hey, isn't it great we can send authors we enjoy little digital notes? Social Media isn't all bad, folks!). Thus began a mutual admiration society between myself and Seán, which culminated with me getting a sneak preview of the book you're holding in your hands right now (be it in the old paper format or on a newfangled digital device. Hey, they both work, trust me).

The Blackening is the kind of book (bringing my thought train back to the station, as it were) that you'd love to go see at a Drive-In Theater.

Does it have horror? Hell yeah, it does.

What about sci-fi? Yup, in spades!

Aliens? Maybe, I'm not here to spoil stuff (but I wouldn't bet against it!).

Is there action and romance and adventure and cults and anti-heroes and villains and damsels in distress and guys in distress and blood and guts and slime and volcanoes and caves and monsters???

YES YES YES YES YES!

And isn't that awesome!?

The great Joe Lansdale, whose genre work is very comparable to O'Connor, actually wrote a series of novels titled *The Complete Drive-In*, a series of novels about all the great stuff mentioned above. In the collected volume of these books, Lansdale refers to one of the stories as a "B-Movie with blood and popcorn."

I couldn't have said it better myself.

Bottom line, O'Connor is a master of creating fantastic entertainment. Stories with monsters, yes, but the stories also have *heart*. They're stories that make you root for the good guys and *boo* the bad guys, that will make you want to close your eyes at the gross parts (and there are plenty of those—ho boy) and tightly clench the hand of your significant other at the scary parts (yup, lots of them, too).

But hey, I think that's just about enough of the previews, don't you? The dancing cartoon concessions are done singing their song, the car engines have been turned off, your speaker is clipped to the window and the faint whisper of white noise bleeds into your ears. The big screen looming before you is dark as the void, but now flickers with the first early frames of a story that will do it's very best to scare you, to make you jump and squeal.

To give you lots of blood with your popcorn.

So, sit back (or recline on the hood if you'd like), have a sip of soda, and enjoy the show.

Now that I think about it, you might want to leave your seatbelt securely buckled.

The Blackening is about to begin...

Vík, Iceland

The black-sand beach of Vík, two-and-a-half hours' drive from Iceland's capital Reykjavík, was not a traditional spot for lovers to declare their undying adoration for one another, but it did carry a certain charm that appealed to both Ben Foster and Alison Carbery's romantic and adventurous spirits. It had taken Ben months to guide Alison to this moment, and he was pretty sure she remained unaware of his impending proposal, even with them standing in such a beautiful setting.

After travelling all the way from Belfast to spend alone time together – away from the pressures of work – they now had the opportunity to indulge in their passions: photography and blogging. When they arrived in Iceland, six days before, they'd spent most of their time in Reykjavík, eating, drinking, and wandering about without a worry. Ben took snaps, while Alison updated her travel blog, which made the trip all the more worthwhile, with their income increasing with every update posted online. It never ceased to amaze them that their travels were funded by their followers.

He rented a car and drove them to the south of the island so Alison could experience the natural splendour. But, more importantly, so they could attend the first ever Festival of Lights in Vík. In his mind, it would be the perfect setting – alone on an empty beach, the waves of the north Atlantic in the background acting as a soundtrack to their unique moment under a sky of radiant beauty. He was confident her eyes would light up – his beautiful partner overwhelmed by his romantic gesture.

However, on the evening they arrived, overlooking the Reynisdrangar basalt sea stacks, a thick grey cloud filled the sky, with a hazy drizzle falling from the heavens as waves trashed about with the erosive force of the entire ocean crashing against the coastline. The smell of the sea was almost overpowering, with a sulfuric stench hanging in the air. So much so, Alison pinched her nostrils shut as they walked along. However, despite the harsh conditions, the place still carried a sense of awe, and Ben felt grateful for the chance to be alive at this moment.

The soft black volcanic sand shifted beneath their feet as they strolled along. When they reached the entrance to what looked to be a large basalt cave, the stones reminded them both of the Giants Causeway back home. In the dying light, Ben filled her in on some of the local folklore and legends – a topic she had a lot of interest in. He told her how the cave used to be home to two large trolls, then pointed out to where the sea stacks loomed.

"The trolls tried to pull a large ship ashore back in the day, Ally. But the sailors battled hard and managed to resist them all the way until sunrise."

"What happened at sunrise?"

"Well, according to legend, trolls and sunshine don't mix well and they end up being turned into stone. Just like in The Hobbit." He pointed over at the stacks again. "There they are now."

"They're kind of, like... blackened and frozen in time, aren't they?"

"Aye. Forever." He jacked up his shoulders and smiled. "Speaking of forever..." The big moment had arrived to ask the question that had burned in him for weeks now. He plunged his hand into his pocket and searched around for the ring, which he'd removed from its box earlier.

Alison looked at the sea stacks, oblivious to his intentions, the early moon revealing itself through a break in the clouds, lighting up the beach with its pale glow.

He clenched the ring and turned her to face him. Goosebumps popped across his arms and shoulders when he looked into her stunning blue eyes. He cleared his throat, ready to say the words he'd been rehearsing in secret for the last few weeks.

"Ally—"

A sharp sound emitted from inside the cave. He turned to examine the entrance for its origin. Nothing, except the background crash of waves on the shore.

"What was that?" Alison asked, pulling him to her as she linked his arm.

"I'm not sure... Probably just the wind echoing—"

Something shrieked from the darkness and he flinched, and not just because Alison dug her nails into his bicep. He wanted to tell her to let go but then something moved in the cave. Something shifted, the sound like the contents of a beer barrel swashing around during transport.

4

Alison released her grip and wandered towards the opening.

"Ally, what are you doing?"

"It could be a wounded animal or something. Maybe a seal?" She looked back. "Come on."

Annoyed that his big moment was gone, he moved forward, determined to work his way around to asking her again. Sick animal or not, he'd come too far to let this opportunity slip away.

The sound stopped as soon as they stood at the entrance. Ben snorted against the heightened stench of rotten eggs. For all he knew, the noise was probably a natural volcanic occurrence, no doubt familiar to residents of Vík.

With nothing but darkness ahead, Alison used the light on her phone to illuminate the immediate interior. The ceiling was made up of solid rock, with icy stalactites hanging from it, some of which had drops of water dripping from them onto the black sand, forming small stalagmites on the cave floor.

Ben had a bad feeling and tried to pull Alison away, but as they stepped back, something caught his attention – something black, almost oil-like. At first, he thought it was a trick of the light, but on closer inspection, something shifted: an unnatural movement – quick, almost a jerk, as if reacting to the phone's torchlight. A squelching noise filled the space.

He tensed. "What the fuck?" And with that, the high-pitched squealing noise returned, causing both of them to flinch.

The torch beam showed black slime oozing from the walls, forming a puddle that flowed towards them, slithering around stalagmites, over the sand and pebbles and around some of the larger rocks until it stopped at their feet.

Alison bent and directed the light at the strange gooey substance.

"Don't touch it," Ben snapped, "It could be volcanic, like lava."

"Relax, Ben. It's okay. It's some sort of animal, like a big leech or something. It'll be fine if we don't scare it."

"A leech? In bloody Iceland? Ally, please..." Even as he said it, he knew pleading with her was a waste. Alison always did her own thing, and when she became fascinated with something, usually animals, she was the type who *had* to make contact.

She dipped her fingers into the liquid. "It's warm. Wait, it kinda feels like... oil?" Then she straightened, as if stung, her gaze fixed on Ben.

He didn't reply, his face going cold as his focus honed in on what was behind her. When she asked what was wrong, he couldn't respond, his mouth agape.

A yelp escaped her when she turned and saw what had stopped him in his tracks.

The ooze had risen from the ground directly in front of her, as if it was standing, resembling a black cephalopod.

"B-Ben? W-what the...?"

She kept her torchlight on it, the beam shaking. His breath caught when two tentacle-like limbs formed from its sides and extended towards her in what appeared to be an offer of friendship. She glanced back at him, then moved her hand as if to reciprocate, but her action froze halfway. She was about to pull back, when the slime arm shot forward, touched her hand, and flowed over her skin.

"Come on, Ally, let's get the fuck out of here." He stepped forward, his legs shaking, and that's when he noticed blood had started dripping from his nose, "What the fuck–"

"Hold on, Ben, I think it wants to... communicate."

The black lump bubbled and popped, forming a humanoid-like head that jutted forward, as if staring directly at Alison. Without warning, its liquid limbs shot out and wrapped themselves around her waist, pulling her off balance, sending her face-first into the sand. The light from the phone vanished, plunging them into darkness.

7

"Ally!"

Her muffled groans filled his ears and he stepped forward to where he thought he'd last seen her, but she wasn't there. She screamed then, but it came from deeper inside the cavern, and his heart filled with horror at the sound of something being dragged across a rough surface.

"Ally!"

He dropped to his knees and scrambled to find the phone, frantic in his search until he touched it and pulled it from the sand. When he aimed the beam into the darkness, he saw nothing but icy rock and an endless cloak of black. Alison's screams grew fainter with every passing second, but he couldn't figure out which direction they were coming from.

"Ally? Ally!"

His roars echoed around him and his heart hammered, fit to burst as panic surged through him. He kept calling out to her, gasping breaths between sobs, but it was to no avail. She was gone and he was left alone in the ice-cold silence.

ONE

It was without a doubt the most beautiful outpost John Ward had ever laid eyes on, and he'd policed in some charming places, but nothing compared to this. From big cities to rural towns, he'd enforced the law of the land, but in a tranquil – often moody – place like Vík, the need for law simply didn't exist. He sat on the steps of the church high up on the hill, overlooking the sleepy seaside village and the Atlantic Ocean – its white walls and red roof reminding him of the local parish back home in Dublin and the remnants of his former self. So, he figured it was the perfect place to end his life.

As with any such objective, he reckoned an excessive consumption of booze was the best way to begin. Or at least that's what he told himself to justify his actions. He did however, miss the familiar tastes from back home, as any Irishman would. Guinness and Jameson were the big ones, but Flóki and Einstök ale were more than worthy substitutes to help him on his journey into oblivion on a quiet October morning.

There are worse places on this planet to die.

He kept his gaze on the waves crashing against the coast, all the while sipping away on his whiskey. Grey clouds released a hazy rain, dampening the village with a smell of the sea and a soft blanket of morning dew. Despite his fondness for the bottle, each day, without fail, he'd wake at 7 a.m., uniform pressed and ready to wear, badge polished to a fine shine. Most days, he wouldn't recall getting dressed but was glad his muscle memory still guided him. When he policed back in Dublin, a wooden baton was the extent of his artillery but, here in Iceland, he moved about with a Glock 21 holstered at his side, and a Mossberg 500 in the boot of his car.

However, it didn't take long for his routine to become a mundane daily act – unsatisfying and burdensome. Being the Chief Inspector in a village with a population of less than three hundred meant there wasn't a whole lot of police work to do. Most days, he found himself acting as a tour guide for the visitors who made the hamlet a rest stop on their travels from Reykjavík to the East of the island. After enough of this, he'd retire to the only bar in town, the Víkurskáli Grill, if it could be called a bar, being more of a mix between a restaurant, gift shop, and wool factory. It was, however, the central hub, where tourists and locals came to eat, drink, and view the ocean from its large windows overlooking the bay.

Most days, he would pull up a stool and stare out the window while indulging in his newfound tastes, thankful that conversations were normally brief in a place with a constant tourist turnover. Over the last week, he'd dealt with nationalities from all over Europe, America, and Asia, and with the Festival of Lights taking place in the next few days, the influx of visitors would swell, with most hanging around longer than usual. His unofficial *job* boiled down to giving the travelling folk one of two instructions: the road to the left, Reykjavík, or the road to the right, the east. That was the beauty (and curse) of living in a place with only one road running through it – everything seemed to be a matter of left or right, black and white, and this made his decision to kill himself an easy one. With cold steel pressed against his temple, all he had to do was give it a squeeze. But, as with most mornings, he lacked the constitution to follow through on his final act.

"I need a proper drink..." He muttered. *Can't check out of this godforsaken life without a proper drink in me.*

"How are you doing, Inspector?" the barman asked, though it came out as more of a series of grunts as he watched him enter the bar. He stroked his long black beard while gazing out the window as the midday sun disappeared behind cloud. "Did you feel the rumble from below yesterday? I hope it is not Katla waking up, huh?"

Ward parked his rear end on his usual seat, wary of the barman's clear attempt to fish for official information. "I'm grand, and, yeah, I did. Nothing major to report, thankfully. I'll just have the usual." He turned away, an obvious hint that he wasn't in the mood for polite interaction.

"Perhaps Katla is waking up at last?" the barman said again. It was a worry that sat in the back of all the locals' minds, living so close to the large volcano that loomed behind the village. It was said that the mountain erupted every twenty to ninety years. Currently, it hadn't blown in over one hundred years, leaving people on edge every time the Earth shook.

"If that mountain is gonna blow, we'd know well in advance." Ward cleared his throat, aware that his voice was hoarse. "Don't concern yourself."

The barman muttered something in Icelandic to his colleague. Ward didn't catch it, but knew it was a sly remark. He wished he knew more of the language, but struggled with the basics, leaving him alienated and bitter. *Next time I see your hairy mug on the road, I'm going to punch your teeth in.*

Sunlight broke through the thick cloud over the horizon, its beams highlighting every wave the cold North Atlantic whipped up – each queuing to crash against the southern coast with an alluring rawness that still amazed him, even though he'd been looking out at the same spot for the last four long months.

With a large gulp of the single malt burning his throat, he concluded, in dead-certain terms, that today was the day he'd finally meet his maker. He slid the empty glass across the bar and called the barman an *Amadán* – *fool* in Irish – his way of fighting back against the language barrier. Then the door to the eatery opened with a loud bang and a young man stormed in, his movements frantic as he looked around the interior. Ward knew he could only be looking for one person. Him.

"Chief. Come quick, there's been an incident down on the beach!" The squeaky voice of Ingvar

Berg hurt Ward's ears. The wait staff giggled, blatantly mocking the village's new, and only, police cadet, who they'd branded *The Wimp* due to his awkwardness and skinny frame.

Ward wasn't in the humour for a headache, or to be embarrassed. With a sigh, he looked at the cadet. "First of all, Ingvar, stop shouting. Get over here and sit your ass down."

"But, Chief, we've had a call, reports of a murder down on the beach." Heads turned at his raised voice, and a confused, almost panicked chatter rose among the locals and tourists.

"Hang on, kid," Ward shouted back, "what you talking about?" He turned and waved at the crowd. "Calm down, folks. He's had a few energy drinks and is a little over-excited. He'll be widdling on the floor in a minute if he keeps it up."

The joke got a few laughs, but most people's faces showed concern.

"Ugh, the Wimp," the barman muttered in disgust, before turning away to examine the cash register.

Ingvar was only a week into his first job after graduating from college with a degree in science. He was young for a cadet, but looked older than his twenty years, with thin hair, almost balding on top. Ward didn't dislike his soft manner, but it helped that he had a near-fluent level of English. He felt the lad was wasted in a place like Vík, with his naivety and eagerness to impress leaving him open to been taken advantage of – and his lack of filter when it came to discussing official business didn't help.

He kicked into gear, grabbing Ingvar under the arm. "Outside. Now!" The cadet had no choice but to comply.

Outside, grey clouds refused to break and a misty rain pasted Ward's face.

"Alright, kid, calm down. You can't be shouting things like that all over the place. You'll start a panic. Use your head, for God's sake. Now, tell me what's going on."

"We had a call in the o-office. Someone down on the b-beach is reporting a mmm-murder."

Ward tried not to react to the lad's nervous stuttering. "Where? Here in fucking Vík? You're having a laugh?"

"No one is l-laughing, Chief. The call came in five minutes ago and I c-came to get you. We need to respond, yes?"

Ward looked out at the sea once again and drew a deep breath, the edges of his vision blurred by too much whiskey. The stacks of Reynisdrangar split the horizon, a sight he couldn't help admiring. *Fuck it, my date with death will have to wait.* He let out a loud sigh and zipped up his jacket. "Right, you go grab the motor. I'll wait here."

It only took a couple of minutes until a Toyota 4x4 skidded to a stop in front of the bar. He climbed in to find his deputy eager to get started.

"This isn't an episode of CSI, kid. Take it easy. Now, drive."

Their feet sank into the black sand as they trudged along the beach, eventually reaching the reported scene of the crime. A young man was kneeling in front of the cave entrance, his face in his hands, his shoulders shaking as he sobbed and groaned.

A local woman tried her hardest to comfort him, frantically signalling to Ingvar to come over. They exchanged a few words in the native language – Ward didn't understand much of it, secretly content at his ignorance.

"Well?" he asked, eager to get the hell away.

"She says she found him like this earlier this morning, but couldn't get much out of him. Something about a missing or injured girl? Possibly a murder? So, she wrapped a blanket around him and put the call into us." Ingvar shrugged to convey his confusion.

Ward thanked the woman and sent her on her way after having Ingvar inform her that she would be contacted for a statement in due course. As he moved closer, the kneeling man's sobs grew louder.

The guy was a tourist – that much he was sure of. Then he noticed his blood-soaked jacket and jeans.

As soon as the man laid eyes on Ward, he sprang to his feet and hugged him, dropping the blanket and thanking him repeatedly.

"Okay, calm down, son." Ward eased the man back and stared at him. "That accent. Where are you from, mate?"

"Belfast. Hey, you're Irish, too, aren't you? Oh, thank G–G–God for that."

"What's your name?"

"B-Ben. Ben F-Foster," he answered, his teeth chattering, which made Ward suspect he'd been out in the cold all night.

"Are you hurt, Ben?" He pointed to the blood.

The Belfast man shook his head, then his shoulders rattled as sobs spilled out again.

"Relax. We're here now. Take a minute to compose yourself and tell me what happened."

Ben took a shuddering breath and glanced into the cave entrance. "It's Ally."

"Who's Ally?" Ingvar asked.

Ward snapped a *Shut the fuck up*! look at his cadet.

"My wee girlfriend. Alison. She... she likes to be called Ally."

"What about her?" Ward asked, his head thumping from what he reckoned might be an early hangover.

Ben glanced at the cave again. "She was taken last night…"

"Taken?" Ward gritted his teeth. "I know you're in shock, but you need to start spitting out the details, man."

"Aye, sorry. She was t-taken. It's in there." He pointed to the cave. "It came down off the walls and took my wee Ally." Then he broke down in floods of tears, repeating her name over and over.

Ward itched for another drink, the only thing that would get rid of his headache. He grabbed Ben and pulled him close so their foreheads almost touched. "I'm not in the mood for games, Mister Foster. Who took her? What happened here?"

"Chief, relax," Ingvar said, his voice shaking.

"Know your place, cadet." He locked eyes with Ben. "This boyo is gonna talk and tell me why he has me down here? We find you here covered in blood… you better start making some sense, lad."

"Let go of me. Didn't you hear me? Ally was taken into the cave last night."

Ward tightened his grip. "By whom?"

"I d-don't know. I don't know what I saw."

Ward held firm as the Belfast man squirmed. "So you said. What? Did some Viking-looking cunt come down here and steal your girl? Left you with a bloody nose, is that it?" As soon as the last word left his mouth, a sickening whiskey belch followed.

"Let go of me, please. You're hurting my arm, so you are."

"I will, when you tell me what the fuck is going on. Where is the girl this woman is talking about? Why is she calling us reporting a murder? What did you do, Foster?"

"Please—"

"Chief!" Ingvar placed his hand on Ward's shoulder.

Ward shrugged him off. "Get your hand off me, boy. Arrest this lad."

"For what?" Ben asked, his brows knitted into a deep frown. "I didn't do anything. What about my Ally?"

Ward ground his teeth again, seconds away from losing it.

Ingvar stepped in between them and grabbed Ben's wrists. "Relax, Mister Foster. We're just going to bring you in, have you cleaned up, and take a statement. It's not a big deal."

Ward snorted and wiped sweat from his brow. "Take him in, Ingvar. And seal off the scene." He stormed back towards the Toyota.

"I didn't do anything, Mister," Ben called after him. "I swear it." But Ward didn't respond, intent on getting away before his anger got the better of him.

TWO

With the cave closed off to the public, rumours swirled around the village – most of which were cast aside as nonsense. Despite this, some tourists couldn't help but be intrigued. So, later that evening, a French father and son trekked across the black sand, ignoring the police tape and signs. Little motivation was needed for a unique set of photographs, and with about an hour of daylight left, they stood at the cave entrance and admired its splendour. Behind them, a light breeze blew, adding nicely to the calming sounds of the sea.

The father assured his son that they were safe in this isolated place, once they kept their wits about them. The young man, his face riddled with acne, which he'd failed to cover with a patchy dark beard, set up a tripod and camera down near the encroaching tide, facing the cave. While he tinkered with the settings, his father made his way to the cave entrance and test-posed with the impressive basalt columns in the background.

After a few rotation shots, the son went to take his turn. He was excited as he approached, eager to climb up the basalt rocks to get a cool new photo for his Instagram. Once settled, he signalled to his father that he was ready.

His father went to the camera and started snapping away, adjusting the filter and zoom settings, while his son smiled and made silly poses.

The wind picked up, blowing grains of sand onto the lens. The father signalled a halt while he cleaned it. Once he was satisfied, he returned to take a few more shots before calling it a day. However, when he placed his eye at the viewfinder, his son was no longer in the same spot. Instead, he had moved deeper into the cave, which is when the father noticed that he was struggling to free himself from something on the wall.

The young man cried for help in French, but his words were barely audible from within the cave.

Panicked thoughts flooded the father's head. Had an animal taken hold of him? Had he fallen and was now caught on a jagged rock? Without hesitation, he dropped everything and ran towards the cave, knocking the camera over, the lens cracking against a rock.

He pounded across the sand, his chest heavy as he gasped for breath. His son's cries became clearer as he reached the entrance. From there, the boy appeared to be hanging or swinging from near the cavern's ceiling.

As the father's eyes adjusted to the darkness, the horror of the situation revealed itself.

The wall was alive.

And whatever it was had his boy, like a fly stuck to a spider's web. But instead of a spider coming to catch its prey, the wall pulsated, and with every throb, his son was pulled deeper into the darkness.

The father screamed reassurances, but was unable to react fast enough. He picked up a stone and threw it towards the black slimy substance. The rock stuck for a moment, then disappeared into the sludge. Seconds later, it came spinning back, narrowly missing his head. His response was rapid – he raced towards the wall, using a basalt column to propel himself upward, before catching hold of the boy's legs. He hung there for a couple of seconds before gravity took them towards the ground, but the goo would not let go of the boy, elasticising as they descended.

"I've got you", he shouted over and over in French.

The boy didn't reply. Above his head, from within the sludge, a slit appeared, showcasing a set of sharp black teeth.

"Aide-Moi—"

Before the boy could finish his plea, their bodies hit the floor.

The father scrambled from his back onto all fours and grabbed hold of his son. At first, he was happy to have the boy in his arms, but his sons face was pale so he shook him to evoke a response. Nothing. Then his skin went cold when he realised that, from his shoulder to ribs, there was nothing but a corrugated wound, resembling a shark-attack victim, with bits of gnarled bone protruding from the mess where his arm used to be.

Bile surged into his throat before he released it with a scream of terror that reverberated through the cavern.

In the depths of despair and confusion, he failed to notice the black slime oozing down the cave walls, until two tentacle-like limbs shot forward from the pooled sludge and wrapped around the boy's remaining arm and a leg. Seconds later, he only had one limb left as the others were torn and sucked into the ebony gloop.

He stood back in shock at the sight of what remained of his boy, unable to look away as his son's remains were whipped into the belly of the cave.

Left with no other choice but to stay, die, or run, he turned and scarpered for the beach.

The smell of the sea and eerie stillness at the mouth of the cave did nothing to ease his panic. He screamed at the top of his lungs for help, in French and English in case there were other tourists close by, but his cries seemed to vanish into the waves before him.

He frantically zipped his jacket up against the cold and stepped towards the broken camera, only to be stopped in his tracks when his son called to him. When he turned, his boy was standing there, full-bodied, arms extended, as if waiting for a hug.

The father couldn't believe his eyes. Was this really happening? Had he dreamed the horror? He wiped a tear from his face, took a step forward, but stopped when everything fell silent, as if the sounds of the sea and wind had been sucked out of the scenario. Then the boy exploded into a cloud of black slime, which coalesced and shot towards him, so fast he had no time to move before it covered both his legs. Whatever monster inhabited the darkness of the cave, it now had him in its grasp, its strength taking him by surprise.

"Aide moi! Help me! Please..."

His screams went unanswered. It was too late. The slime pulsated, almost covering him now as it dragged him deep into the dark.

THREE

The police station was nothing more than a small weather-beaten log cabin with a green roof that sat in front of the only football pitch in Vík. Inside was open plan, with Ward's desk in the corner, with a large map of the Southern Region hanging on the wall behind it.

Ben sat on a chair, handcuffed and upset.

Ward parked himself behind the desk and took a swig from a flask he'd hidden away in the top drawer. He grimaced as the whiskey burned his neck on the way down. Fuck what anyone thought, it was the only way to ease his thumping headache. He held the flask on his lap, his curiosity about the Belfast man piqued. Since arriving in Vík, this was the first real call he'd had to deal with and he wanted to know all the details before the larger stations in Selfoss or Reykjavík got word.

"Okay, Mister Foster... from Belfast..." He took another sour mouthful while reviewing Ben's passport. "Tell me exactly what happened last night."

"Like I said, something came at us in the cave..."

"So, you both were attacked?"

"Aye. It wasn't threatening... at first."

"It?" Ingvar said. "So, we are talking about some sort of animal here?"

Ward threw another death stare his way.

"No," Ben answered, "*It* was something else. It looked like some sort of giant leech. Oil-like, if that makes sense?"

"Ha," Ward barked. "Were you taking drugs or alcohol by any chance?"

Foster frowned, looking from Ward to his flask. "I'm serious, mate. It came from inside the cave." He looked up at the map, his gaze distant, as if recalling the horror over again in his mind. "At first, it moved really fast, making crazy screeching sounds, then it just sort of flowed across the sand, stopping at our feet. Ally touched it, and as soon as she made contact with it..." He trailed off, flicking glances from one wall to the next, even behind him. "Before I knew what was happening, she was face down in the dirt." His shoulders shook and he shut his eyes, but he seemed to pull himself together, swallowed hard, and looked directly at Ward. "It was dark, but I heard her screams as she was dragged off into the cave."

The cabin became silent until Ingvar grunted and stepped away from the window. "So, we're dealing with, err... a shadow—"

"And the blood?" Ward asked, his flask stalled below his mouth.

"Aye, well, she stood in front of me. I couldn't move a muscle. Well, I'm not gonna lie – I froze. And the piercing sound filled my head causing my nose to bleed. The blood gushed like someone had turned on a tap."

"Anything else?"

He shook his head as he shrugged, then let out a long sigh. "That was pretty much it until that lady found me. I must have passed out from the shock or something. Then you lads came along."

"That beach is pitch black at night," Ingvar said. "Why were you there?"

"We went down hoping the skies would clear up. I was going to wait until the Northern Lights party to do it, but the setting was just so perfect. So, I tried to do it last night instead."

Ward lowered his flask and leaned forward. "Do what?"

"Come on, mate, you know what."

Ward got to his feet and slammed his free hand down on the desk top. "So the woman on the beach was right then – you killed the girl. What did you do with her body?"

"No, you fucking lunatic. Fucking peelers are always jumping to conclusions, aren't ye?" He looked at Ingvar, as if expecting him to agree with him. "I was going to ask her to be my wife. It was supposed to be the perfect proposal."

Ward looked at Ingvar, who raised both eyebrows.

Ben shifted in his chair. "Sure, why else do young people come to this island?" He hung his head and the sobs came. "I love her so much. What am I supposed to do now?" He straightened, eyes wide. "Ye have to help me find her!"

Ward signalled to Ingvar to head outside. "And he calls me a lunatic. Ben, you just stay right here and pull yourself together."

He followed Ingvar out to the porch. "Okay, you go back in there and get all that nonsense into an official statement, yeah? Don't, under any circumstances, let him leave, and hold onto his passport. He's either on drugs or a murderer... or a mental patient, or maybe all three?"

"Okay, no problem, Chief. I'll do what I can. What are you going to do?"

"I'm going for a drink. I need to think on this for a while."

"Don't you think you've had enough—"

"Enough what?" Ward snapped, his fist clenched.

Ingvar stepped back and held his hands out. "We've... a situation here—"

"Mind your tongue. Don't ever question me, boy." He hitched his trousers up and zipped up his jacket. "I've dealt with bigger problems than this in my time. Now do as you're told. That's an order."

"What can we charge him with?"

"Nothing for now. There is about an hour of daylight left. I'll go back to the beach in a while. I need to check out the cave. If he killed her, I'll find something. I have to trust my hunch." He stretched out the cricks in his back. "I hope to Christ I'm wrong on this."

"So, you think he did it?"

"After hearing that story of his, I think there's something wrong with his head. Oil? Leeches? A woman taken by the night? Bloody noses caused by some sort of sensory attack? Ramblings of a madman, Ingvar. The Northies are all a bit like that back home. Melodramatic, but sometimes a poetic bunch." He took a quick look outside, then shook his head. "Right, I'll be back in a while."

Ward parked up outside the cave entrance and sat in the Toyota, trying to make sense of everything that had allegedly happened. Daylight was fading fast and, as he looked into the darkness beyond the large basalt columns, he feared what he might find inside. Images of a young girl lying dead on the rocks, filled him with anger, apprehension, and a deep sadness that gripped his heart. Unwanted memories flashed through his head, and he struggled to maintain his focus.

His breathing came heavy, and he didn't like the wheeze emanating from deep within his chest. Guilt smothered him, which was nothing new considering he'd failed to leave his conscience back in Dublin. It took a huge amount of effort to clear his mind, grounding himself by focusing on the sounds of the shore. The whiskey helped but, also, didn't.

The view was spectacular: the sea, the green-black hills; the large glacier, Mýrdalsjökull, looming over the village. A heady volcanic stink filling the air – a combination of sulphur and... something else he couldn't get a handle on.

He slapped the dash at his inability to clear his mind. He'd come all this way to cleanse what was left of his soul – to die peacefully in the dark – but couldn't stop thinking about Niamh – his daughter. *I'd never leave her alone in a cave.* He let out a long, wheezy sigh, figuring he owed Alison that much.

As he shoved the driver's door open, a gust of icy wind shot in, making him flinch. Apart from wanting to end it all, feeling vulnerable was not in his DNA, but thoughts of what he might find filled him with dread. He headed across the beach, his boots crunching the coarse sand as he hurried towards the cave, the wind stinging his ears. Then he noticed something sticking up from the sand. Upon inspection, he realised it was a tripod – the attached camera damaged by rock and water. Nonetheless, his instinct was to carry it with him.

At the entrance, he found himself staring into a black hole that led into the depths of the earth. By his feet, evidence of a struggle was etched into the black sand.

I'm doing this for you, Alison. You need me, just like my beautiful Niamh did.

He swallowed a swig of whiskey, took a deep breath, fixed his jacket, switched on his torch and without knowing what he might find, headed into the cave.

FOUR

Daylight blazed when he opened his eyes. He stirred, blinked a few times, and tried to place himself. It wasn't too difficult, even on the hard end of a drunk night. Who could mistake the *kip* they'd placed him in? He moved, but pulled back when his head spun and his stomach lurched. Bile filled his mouth, and he just about managed to roll over before he emptied the night's contents onto the floor.

The sunlight brought an unusual amount of heat for this time of year. He looked up at the window, the action bringing on a fit of coughing that continued until he could hardly breathe. "Well, fuck me..."

Ward wasn't ready to face the world. Not even his muscle memory was kicking in. In fact, he resented the very thought of being alive. From the moment he'd set foot in Iceland, his nights had regularly involved drinking hard liquor in the isolation of his room, and staring at his Glock. He'd bite back the whiskey and try to figure out the best spot to place the muzzle. Would putting one through his temple be the quickest? One in the mouth? Under his chin?

Despite the dark thoughts, the fear of botching the job meant the trigger was never pulled – he couldn't envisage himself cooped up in a hospital bed for weeks, being brought back to health after failing to blow his head off. This allowed him to explore other ways to do the deed, with hanging and car crashing winning over drowning and cliff falls. As he lay on the floor now, feeling like he'd been steam-rolled by a locomotive, his matt-black handgun once again looked like the most viable option – it even had a round in the chamber, ready to go. Could he do it?

Who would even miss me? The people around here certainly wouldn't. They despise me. An Irishman running their show? Ha! So, who does that leave me with? Ingvar? The boy has some growing up to do, but he could do a lot better than be stuck with the likes of me.

He reached for the gun and pressed it against his temple, squeezing the trigger enough to release the safety. Tears prickled his eyes and he blinked them away. *I couldn't save you. If only I could have saved you. My baby girl. You were my world. Fuck it...*

Deep breath held, he closed his eyes and applied the final pressure to the trigger.

The bang came before he completed the action, and he opened his eyes to a flurry of knocks and thumps on his front door.

"Chief! Chief! Are you in there?" The unmistakable squeak of the cadet. "Open up, Chief. Please!"

"Ah, for fuck's sake." He sighed. "Hold your fucking horses."

He placed the handgun back in the holster hanging from the chair. As he scrambled to his feet, he caught his reflection in the mirror and was disgusted by what faced him: his tossed hair, his mottled, rotund gut overhanging the elastic on his boxer shorts; his eyes, tired and sullen.

Dragging his trousers on almost proved fatal as he stumbled across the floor, cursing and grumbling as he went. He got to the door and unlocked it. Sunlight poured in around the cadet's silhouette. The lad was always prim, proper, and ready for duty, and as soon as Ward laid eyes on him, whispers of the day and night before came back to him. *Fuck, I have to sort this drink shit out. I need to get a handle on it.*

"What do you want, kid?" he asked. "My head is pounding and I'm in no mood for your bullshit today."

"Chief, you never came back last night."

Ward scratched his stubbled jaw, drawing a blank. "So? What's it to you?"

"So, I was worried. I had to keep Ben Foster in the station overnight. I came looking for you this morning and the barmen at the Grill said you went there last night and... and they had to put you to bed?"

"Yeah, well, I wasn't in the mood for Foster's crap, and they shouldn't be talking about my personal affairs."

"I was worried. I-I thought something might have happened to you, so I went to look for you in the cave this morning."

Ward remained silent, taking the time to recall his steps before he'd gone so far as to not remember. He squinted against the light flaring around his apprentice. "I'm assuming you found the same thing as I did then?" He hacked something raw out of his throat and spat past Ingvar, who cringed at the act.

"If you mean rocks, sand, and ice hanging from the ceiling, then yeah." He shrugged. "I guess you found... nothing."

Ward nodded, then pressed his tired eyes. "You know what this means, don't you?"

"No. What?"

"We let that little Northie prick take us for a ride with his bullshit talk. Black oil? Giant leeches? Random nosebleeds? It's all a load of crap. We're in the back-arse of Iceland, for God's sake. The loser was probably on the comedown from an acid trip or something."

"But, Chief, I checked his flight records. He did travel here with a woman by the name of Alison Carbery. She has an address in Belfast and the pair of them have valid UK passports."

"Oh." A sharp pain stung the back of Ward's eyes as everything spun. "Then it seems we have a genuine missing-person's case. And one witness." He turned to search for his shoes and shirt, and saw the puke-covered heap on the floor. "Fuck it, you go get the car, kid. I need to clean myself up."

"Where we going?"

"Ben Foster needs more questioning."

He slammed the door in the cadet's face, then ran for the bathroom, his mouth full to bursting before he reached the toilet pot.

Ben Foster's wrist was raw from being cuffed to the radiator, having spent the night on the floor of the police cabin. The shock and horror of the previous day and night before had settled somewhat, though he still couldn't believe what had happened to his poor Ally, and now he sat in a state of frustrated anger, watching the door swing open with a loud bang.

Ward stormed in, his glare fierce. He pulled a chair across the floor and parked it backwards in front of Ben, then threw his leg over and sat, arms folded, staring. His breathing came heavy, and the large exhales from his nose had Ben worrying that maybe this guy was going to get physical.

"Well, big man," he said, "what's going on? Any news of my Ally?"

Ward just stared hard at him. And he kept at it for what felt like ages, then pulled a bottle of water from his pocket and sat up. "Listen to me, Mister Foster. You're going to tell me everything. You've had plenty of time to clear that head of yours and you're not leaving this godforsaken island until I am satisfied with what you have to say. Do you understand me?"

"Fuck that, mate. I just want to find my Ally. I've been cuffed in this office for the whole night. What's been happening? It's been roughly a day and half now. Any sight or sound of her?"

"I'll do the asking here, lad."

"Aye. Well, if you're not going to answer my questions, how about letting me go somewhere to piss? And I'm starving. Any chance of some food?"

Ward just stared, his requests falling on deaf ears.

Jesus, why am I being treated like this? His chest tightened at the memory of Ally's screams as she was dragged into the darkness. "Jesus Christ, we need to be doing something!"

Ward cleared his throat, "I'll start. Ben Foster, twenty-eight years old, from Belfast, Ireland. Correct?"

"Well, Northern Ireland, but aye, that's correct."

"Queen's man, are you? Right, well, you travelled here ten days ago with Alison Carbery. Twenty-six years old, also from Belfast?"

"Aye. That's right, mate. We came down here for the Festival of Lights."

"The night before last, you two were on Reyna... Reynisfar... Fara–"

"Reynisfjara." Ingvar offered.

"Whatever. The fucking black-sand beach, and she was attacked by what you called 'an oily leech', then she was dragged off into the cave by this, eh... black blob?"

Ben shuffled on the floor. "Aye. You make me sound crazy when you put it like that, but, aye, that's the way of it."

"You can see my problem here, Ben, can't you?"

"Aye, I suppose I do. But you have to see my problem, too. Where's my Ally? What the fuck has happened to her? And why aren't you out searching for her?"

The phone on the desk rang. Ward signalled to his cadet to answer it. The guy spoke in Icelandic, while his boss kept his gaze locked on Ben, as if studying his face for signs of guilt. Then he guzzled down the entire contents of the water bottle before releasing a satisfied moan, as if rejuvenated. *Jesus Christ, this fat fuck hardly thinks I've done Ally in, does he?* He looked around the cabin's interior. "Can I ask you a question, mate? How did a Jackeen end up working in a place like this? You're a long way from Dublin."

"Mind your tongue," Ward snapped. "I... wanted to come here."

"Yeah? A holiday, is it? I'd say it's some switch from The Big Smoke."

Ward didn't react, just glared, as if sizing him up. A part of Ben understood the man's frustration, while, on the other hand, he resisted every urge to smash his whiskey-nosed face.

"Chief, we have to go back down to the beach."

Ben sat up, goosebumps erupting on his arms at the sight of the cadet's face turning pale.

Ward looked at the lad. "Why, what's happened?"

"What's going on?" Ben asked. "Is it my Ally?"

"Shut up, you!" Ward snapped.

"Another incident, Chief."

"Same place?"

"Yes."

"Fuck."

Ben sat stunned as Ward warned him to sit and be quiet, then linked his cadet under his arm and pulled him towards the door, ordering him to go get the car.

"What about me?" Ben shouted. "Any chance of some food?" He pulled at the radiator. "Hey, come on! What about my Ally?"

Ward tossed the empty plastic bottle at him. "Here, piss in that. We'll be back in a while."

On the beach, a small crowd had gathered behind the police barriers Ingvar had set up the day before. Ward and his cadet pushed their way through and stumbled upon what everyone was trying so hard to get a look at – dismembered body parts strewn across the sand, severed and torn, and blue from the cold. Thankfully, for them, the barrier had done its job and kept the small group from seeing the full extent of the horror.

They acted fast, corralling the crowd from the beach back to the car park, then reinforcing the barriers with police tape and assured everyone that it was nothing more than the remains of some animal washed up on the shore.

Next, they proceeded to examine the body parts.

"Is this Alison?" Ingvar asked.

"I don't think so." Ward replied, pointing to what looked like the remains of a male hand.

"Did you not see any of this last night?"

"No," Ward snapped. "Granted it was nearly dark, but I would have seen this."

"It's like these were put through a meat grinder and spat out," Ingvar said, his horror at the sight before them obvious in his shaking voice and demeanour.

Ward didn't reply, unable to pull his attention from the traces of black goo that covered the severed limbs. "This shit is beyond our expertise, lad." With a long-drawn sigh, he shook his head. "I'm going to have to call this in."

As much as he hated dealing with his superiors, the situation had moved out of his control. He dreaded the thought of putting a call into Reykjavík and speaking with the commissioner, but with two serious incidents in less than forty-eight hours, what choice did he have? Whatever happened here was beyond anything he'd experienced, filling his already pained gut with an unease he didn't like one bit.

Ingvar edged closer and cleared his throat. "I know you don't want to deal with the commissioner, but may I make a suggestion, Chief?"

"What's that, kid?" Ward asked, failing to hide his air of despondency.

"I know a girl in the Natural Sciences department in the University who might be able to help."

Ward didn't reply, his gaze drifting out towards the sea.

"Sir, I'm in agreement with you. Someone or something did this. We are dealing with an animal or some sort of fucked-up serial killer. This girl may be able to help. I went to school with her – she has a big interest in debunking strange phenomena. If I call her, she could be here in a few hours. Convince her to draft up a report, then, at least, that way you have something of substance before calling the commissioner. It'd keep our asses covered for not calling this in yesterday."

Ward nodded. "My gut is telling me we're dealing with something bigger than some crazed lunatic. But maybe you're right. Give me her number and I'll call her."

He entered it in his phone and wandered back towards the Toyota. The situation was bizarre. How was he going to explain it to a complete stranger? Still, it might be worth a try – as mad as it would sound, it was better than bringing the whole brigade down from the capital. And he had to trust his gut. No matter how odd it all felt, he knew deep down that something strange, perhaps otherworldly, was going on.

FIVE

Rakel Atladóttir could barely keep her eyes open at the university's science-committee meeting. After a night of heavy drinking, the last thing she wanted to deal with was listening to other members talk about how they could squeeze more funding from the Research and Doctoral projects. The meetings seemed to roll around every few weeks, always covering the same issues, and making her feel like she was living in a perpetual Groundhog Day. So, when her phone buzzed, she jumped at the opportunity to leave the conference room and rushed out to the corridor to take the call. Anything was better than being subjected to such constant boredom, especially when her mind kept shifting back to the bitter break-up she'd been struggling to recover from over the past few weeks.

She woke up one morning to find her boyfriend missing from their bed. His things had been cleaned out and all that remained was a spitefully worded *Dear John* letter on her kitchen table. It said that he couldn't be with her anymore because she held him back, as he wasn't ready to settle down and wanted to travel. Her heart broke – she'd been convinced he was the one, and hoped that wherever he was, he was miserable for leaving her in such a horrible way.

Despite her friends telling her that she shouldn't be drinking as much as she had been over the last few weeks, she did it anyway. With her physical health noticeably deteriorating, her skin blotchy, and her body weight dropping to just under seven stone, it seemed that drink was the only substance that held her together.

She checked to see if the hallway was clear. "H-Hello?"

"Hello. Am I speaking with Ms Atla... dot... tear?" a man asked, his struggle to pronounce her surname obvious but unsurprising from someone not Icelandic.

"Atladóttir," she corrected, relieved that it wasn't her ex calling. "And, yes, you are. Who am I talking to?" At the same time, she was a bit disappointed.

"Forgive the cold call. My name is John Ward. Well, Inspector W–Ward."

"Oh, hello. How can I help you? Am I... in some sort of trouble, Inspector?" Could this be a prank from her ex?

"No, not at all. You were recommended by Ingvar Berg. He is my deputy here in Vík. There is something I'd like to speak to you about, if I could steal a few minutes of your time?"

She agreed and listened – entertaining a cold call was better than struggling through the meeting with a banging headache. The incidents down in Vík came as a shock and, although she knew Ingvar, it was all too sudden to fully grasp.

"No one outside of Vík is aware of this yet," the inspector explained. "We've kept it all under wraps for now. I don't want to cause a panic with the Festival of Lights coming up. Which is why I need your help. Without sounding harsh, I'm hoping that an animal has done this and it's not the work of a crazed person. Maybe you could lend your experience to the situation? Ingvar speaks very highly of you..."

Rakel looked up and down the hallway. *This has to be a prank. Surely?*

The inspector continued his reasoning and mentioned Ingvar again. She asked to speak to her old friend to confirm the request, and when she was convinced that everything checked out and was legit, she agreed to drive down to Vík.

Ward cursed the headache swirling around in his head, but that didn't stop him sipping from his flask. He yearned for a quiet day, where he could perhaps slip off somewhere and never return – where he could finally squeeze the trigger, sending hot lead through his head to achieve his ultimate release. However, dark thoughts and suicide plans would have to wait, with this calling from deep inside too strong to ignore. Also, the prospect of some real police work made him feel alive, almost invigorated, and despite the depression that made his gun look so attractive, he somehow managed to shelve his inner demons and focus on the task at hand.

The scientist arrived at the beach just before sunset, where she was greeted by Ward, Ingvar, and a burst of icy rain. Shielding her face with her hands, she ran from her car to the police vehicle. After taking time to shake off the cold, she introduced herself with a limp handshake and a friendly *how have you been* chat with Ingvar. While the pair got reacquainted, Ward found himself staring at her in the rear-view mirror. He liked her long, dyed-red hair and casual-dress sense, which triggered uncalled-for memories of his ex-wife.

As the pair rambled on in Icelandic, Ward's mind drifting unexpectedly into sexual fantasy – something he hadn't experienced in a long time. And just as he was about to immerse himself, she tapped his shoulder.

"What exactly are we dealing with here, gentlemen?"

Ward halted Ingvar's response with a sharp elbow to the ribs.

"Well, the reason I called you, Rakel, is because what you're about to see is beyond bizarre. In all my years of police work, I've never seen human remains in the state we have discovered these poor bastards in."

"How do you mean, Inspector?"

"Let's just say they were disposed like... unwanted rubbish. Whoever done this, left the remains at the cave entrance, perhaps to send a message, or a warning. Christ, we're lucky this shit hasn't gone all virus by now."

"You mean viral?"

Ward shot her a look. He didn't like being corrected, even if it was by a cute scientist. "Look, whatever the reason, it's what we found on the remains that has us perplexed the most."

"And what is that?"

"Slime. Gooey and black. Almost like an oily tar." He glanced in the rear-view mirror and looked away when his gaze met hers. "I've seen serial killers leave calling cards before. And I've seen dismembered bodies before, but that was gang-related back home, like a trademark kind of thing. And I highly doubt there are any drug cartels roaming around this place, so whoever this prick is, he wants the media to know his sign."

When she didn't reply, he looked in the mirror. Her eyes were closed, as if she was trying to visualise the scene in her mind.

"You believe we are dealing with a person here?" she asked.

"Yeah. Or maybe an animal..."

"There are no indigenous predators around Vík that could do such a thing, Inspector. Except maybe a polar bear, but they never come this far south. Even if they did, under extreme circumstances, it would be due to hunger, and anything they find to eat, would be consumed. Of course, this is only my opinion." She looked at the rain pelting off the window. "A serial killer is a whole different ball game."

They waited for the shower to let up. Once it did, she was escorted to the crime scene.

The coastal wind cut into them, the sea spray showering them in a salty haze, stinging Rakel's lips and eyes. The conditions were not ideal for examining dead bodies, but she got on with the job, ignoring the weather as best she could.

Ingvar and Ward left her at the scene to go wait in the car, with the warning not to go unaccompanied into the cave. They figured having fresh eyes without distractions would work best.

At first, the sight of the limbs upset her. *What could have done such a thing?* She concluded that the violence was not that of an animal. Someone did this with some sort of tool. There could be no other plausible explanation. As she pulled the tarp back over the remains, a sound from inside the cave caught her attention – a fast-dripping noise. She braced herself for a gush of water but nothing came, other than silence beneath the wind and crashing surf.

She figured it was just the wind echoing inside the cave. As she went to turn away, something caught her eye – a strange movement on one of the limbs – something pulsating, as if it was breathing.

53

On closer inspection, she noticed small pockets of goo clumped around the severed wounds, vibrating, almost bubbling. It was the strangest thing she'd ever seen. With practiced efficiency, she reached into her bag and retrieved a glass jar, a pair of vinyl gloves, and a cotton swab. The sample was stringy and gooey, like a lump of honey falling from a spoon, only this was black and oily. She managed to gather a decent amount into the jar before pocketing it. Then she wiped her brow and hurried towards the Toyota, with so many questions running through her mind.

"Well? What do you think?" the inspector asked, not giving her a chance to settle into the back seat.

"I think your gut is right, Inspector Ward. I think you need to contact your superior."

"So, this wasn't an animal?"

"No. The wounds were made with precision. An instrument had to have been used."

"And what about the slime?"

"As you said, a calling card of some sort," she answered, hoping her lie wasn't seen in her eyes.

They sat in silence, the rain lashing against the windows.

"So, what happens now?" Ingvar asked, looking from one to the other.

Rakel shrugged. "As soon as this rain breaks, I'm going back to Reykjavík. This is outside my area of expertise."

Ward watched the scientist hop into her car and head back on the road west, disappearing beneath heavy rainfall that blurred the darkening horizon. Nothing inside compelled him to stop her. What was the point in even bringing her out here to analyse something he already knew the answer to? Whatever he was about to face from his superiors no longer mattered. His job was in Vík, and his duty was to protect the village at all costs, He shook his head. *Of all the places in the world for trouble to find me, it had to be here, in the middle of fucking nowhere.*

"Ingvar, call a meeting for first thing in the morning. We have to put this village on alert."

"The commissioner won't be happy if he is not consult—"

"I don't care about him."

"And what about the festival? If you put Vík on alert for a killer on the loose, they'll cancel it. And that will cost the village a lot of revenue."

"People are dying. I can't risk more lives."

"I know, Chief, but—"

"Assemble the townsfolk, Ingvar. This is not a fucking drill."

SIX

Rakel's ID badge allowed her access to the university's laboratory despite the late hour. She couldn't wait to start working on the sample and thought about it the whole journey back from Vík. In her mind, she struggled to shed the image of the black, oily substance clinging to the severed limbs. What was it? Where did it come from?

After parking close to the university, but far enough away to avoid being spotted by CCTV cameras, she made a quiet entrance through the rear of the building. She placed the glass jar on the professor's table and examined it. The liquid appeared to be in a solid state.

The urge to open the jar ate away at her, but she managed restraint, deciding to hit the vending machines for a can of Coke first – the sugar rush would keep her awake. As she gulped down the fizzy drink, she noticed the clock on the wall – two minutes to midnight. Then she thought about her lab partner. *Would Rúnar be awake at this hour? He needs to see this. It can't wait until the morning.* With a quick swipe on her smart-phone screen, she dialled his number.

"Come on, Rúnar, please, please pick up," she muttered while waiting to connect.

To her joy, he eventually answered with a groggy "Hello?"

"Rúnar, it's Rakel."

"Huh? Rakel? What time is it? Are you okay?" His voice came dry and hoarse.

"I'm fine–"

"Is it that boyfriend again? These late-night calls are becoming regular–"

"Just shut up and listen to me. I need you to come to the lab."

"What? Are you crazy? It's the middle of the night..."

"I know what time it is. I wouldn't call if it wasn't important. Now, listen." She didn't have time to argue so proceeded to describe the events of the day and what she had in her possession. At first, he asked was she drunk again and playing a prank on him but, eventually, her persistence won him over.

"Okay," he eventually agreed, groaning out through a long yawn, "I'll be there within the hour."

Rúnar Bergsson was a brute of a man, who wore his hair and beard long. He had a thing for flannel shirts, often resembling a rustic lumberjack, which wasn't the typical look for a college professor in the university. Even so, it didn't stop him winning the respect of his peers and students. Rakel and he were close friends, and the students loved it when the pair conducted a lecture together. She had the mind for science and reason, while he liked to speculate, which earned him a reputation for outlandish theories, and soon they got tagged with the nicknames *Mulder and Scully*.

About an hour later, he arrived at the lab to find Rakel in an excited state. He couldn't recall the last time he'd seen her this animated, but figured it had to be for a good reason considering the late hour.

"Okay, crazy lady, this better be good," he shouted on entering the room. He slammed the door shut. "If we're caught in here at this time…"

Rakel didn't acknowledge his remark, ushering him over to the table. "Come here, quick. You have to see this."

He indulged her. She had four petri dishes in a line, each containing a black liquid. He waited for the punchline, but it never came. Instead, he listened to her spout out theories about the substance and its origin. It was at this point he realised she was one-hundred percent serious about the discovery. Normally, with Rakel, she'd be jumping through hoops trying to debunk something like this – the change in character confusing him.

"Okay, Rakel, you need to slow down here and tell me what the fuck this stuff really is? Where did it come from? And why you are so pumped up about it?"

"Rúnar, I told you, it came from the body of a dead person. The police down in Vík think it might be a serial killer's calling card, or something like that, but I've never seen anything like this before."

"What's so special about a lump of goo? And do they know you've taken this sample from a crime scene?"

She glanced at him. "Never mind all of that. All that matters now is that we possess it and have the opportunity to study it while we are the only people who know about it."

The vast amount of information was a lot for him to process, but the one thing that stuck out was the fact that she stole evidence from an active crime scene. A serious offence and something he didn't want to be a part off.

"I'm out, Rakel. You've lost it. We could lose our jobs over this. Dump that shit and let's get out of here."

She shook her head with vigour. "Watch," she said, "just watch..." She moved across the lab to the fridge and removed an ice block, which she placed on the table. Then she pulled a box of matches from her pocket. With a nod, she proceeded to show him her findings. The smell of sulphur rose into the air, the flame flickering under the strong lights. She dropped the burning match into one of the petri dishes, evoking a loud squeal from the liquid when contact was made. Then the substance bubbled, expanding at such a rate that it split the dish in two.

"Holy fuck!" Rúnar shouted. His scalp prickled as an icy wave washed across it.

"I know, right? Wait..." She waved for him to calm down, then picked up the ice cube with a thong and dropped it on the bubbling goo. In an instant, the bubbles popped and the oil receded, breaking into a few droplets.

"Wow. That's a neat magic trick," he said, though he wasn't as impressed with the second experiment.

She stared at him, her eyes wide, almost pleading. "Don't you see what this is?"

All he could do was shrug. "No. Something you figured out using the periodic table?"

With a frustrated grunt, she pushed past him. "Go on then, go home if you don't believe me."

"Believe what, exactly? You haven't told me what or where this stuff is from."

"If I knew that, I wouldn't have called you," she snapped, flustering as she changed her gloves.

He looked down at her and released a contrite sigh. "Ok, I'm sorry for laughing at you. Take me through it again."

It was a long night and the pair worked away on the samples. Time after time, through a variety of experiments, they concluded that cold proved detrimental to 'healthy' function and heat activated it, while extreme heat forced an explosive reaction. However, that was nothing to the discovery they made at 5.30 a.m. They placed small samples into a cage containing two adult rats – one male, one female.

What happened next shocked them beyond belief. The liquid pulsated and slithered about the bottom of the cage, attracting the attention of the rodents.

The male rat, large and white, who Rúnar called *Splinter*, scurried over to the sludge, its whiskers twisting and tweaking as it analysed the foreign substance. Then, to their horror, in a burst of motion, the slime latched onto the rodent with what looked like a gorilla's hand that had the rat squealing and struggling in its grip, unable to free itself.

Rúnar couldn't believe what he was seeing, and only realised Rakel was gripping his arm when her nails dug into his skin.

After about thirty seconds, the slime formed a mouth that revealed sharp black teeth, then proceeded to bite into the rodent. Blood squirted as the substance savaged and consumed its prey before returning to a solid-like and passive state at the bottom of the cage.

"What the fuck?" he said, unable to look away from the blood-spattered cage.

April, the female rat, left its corner to investigate the scene. Rúnar tried to grab her before the sludge sprang up again, but Rakel pulled him back, her eyes telling him not to be stupid. The substance shot forward, but this time the rodent wasn't chewed up. Instead, the slime wrapped itself around her body and proceeding to enter through every orifice, eventually disappearing from view.

The animal stopped struggling and shifted into a docile state, then returned to the corner of the cage without a sound.

"What's happened?" Rakel asked.

"Look!" he said, "her eyes have turned black."

Rakel just stared. "What the...?"

The rat remained still and silent. They monitored her over the next few hours and, to their surprise, the only change was her abdomen swelling. Their conclusion was that the slime reacted aggressively towards males – possibly drawn to certain hormones. Both of them had studied biology at length, and this behaviour was not uncommon with certain species in the animal kingdom. However, this was no animal – it was a sentient lump of sludge.

Rakel lifted the bloated rodent and took a urine sample.

"What are you doing?" he asked.

"Just a standard health check for diseases, pregnancy, you know, things like that..."

"Diseases? She's a clean rat. All our rats are clean in here. What are you hoping to find?"

"Hopefully nothing, but that stuff forced its way inside her for a– Oh, fuck!" She stood back, un-phased at knocking her can of Coke over, pointing to the computer screen.

"What's the matter?"

"You know what that's telling us?"

He scanned the data at a glance. "Em... no. What?"

"I think I get it now. Whatever this stuff is, it sees the male as a threat, while the female of the species, it wants to use reproductively... to possibly advance itself."

"What, like some sort of evolutionary device?" He couldn't help snorting at the hypothesis.

"I think so... because April is going to be a mommy."

SEVEN

Kári Ingason, like all his predecessors, was a hard man, who'd fought aggressively to become the *Ríkislögreglustjóri* – National Police Commissioner. He wore his gold-buttoned black uniform with pride, his authority reaching every corner of the country with a cloak of respect and a shadow of fear. Everyone, the citizens and his peers, acknowledged that he was a man you didn't cross. Despite this, he was recognised as a patriot, who loved his country dearly. He awoke every day with the dream of a better tomorrow for the island, and always worked hard to protect the natural beauty, though he was finding it more difficult to manage this with the rise of budget airlines bringing in a constant flow of tourists. Visitors brought money, and the economy needed every penny it could get, particularly the rural towns and villages – he understood this, and accepted it with an underlining bitterness. When the big economic crash of '08 happened, he was one of the high-profile protesters out calling for the bankers to be jailed. He considered their actions an act of treason against his beloved nation.

Under his watch, crime was at an all-time low. Most mornings, he'd wake up to only two or three emails with something marked for his attention. Nothing major, mostly tourists getting into drunken trouble, or the odd spot of domestic violence. So, when the first email of the day contained: **VÍK ON HIGH ALERT – CURFEW IN PLACE** in the subject line, he couldn't believe his eyes. His initial thought was that Katla had finally erupted, but then he realized there was no way it could have done so without him knowing well in advance.

With a forceful tap on his phone's screen, he opened the email, which detailed Ward's actions down on the south coast, in Vík of all places. His disbelief turned to frustrated anger.

The Festival of Lights was set to be one of the biggest events of the year, and Vík was hosting it for the first time. Several thousand tourists would flock from far and wide to witness the splendour of the Aurora Borealis from the black-sand beach. Gazers would watch the spectacle with wonder, with live music, street food, a proper carnival, and – of more importance to the village – they'd all spend money.

"Fucking idiot," he repeated over his coffee. He composed his thoughts, somehow managing to hold his anger in check. Ward was a disgrace and shouldn't be on the force, but he had taken him on secondment as a favour to the Irish Garda Commissioner, who needed him out of the media glare and away from his duties in Dublin. He didn't care much for the details as long as the *oaf* did what he was told, which was to stay out of sight and keep a low profile for the duration of his stay.

Not much chance of that. When the *fool* arrived on the island, he was warned to stay out of trouble – his reputation preceding him. However, on the second night of duty, the shit hit the fan after he was caught having drunken sex with an English tourist in his car just outside of Reykjavík. The next day, he was relocated to the south of the island and given his final warning: not to come to his attention again.

Kári mulled over the consequences, then, as soon as breakfast was done, he rounded up some of his best men and departed the capital.

Ingvar finished the final report ahead of the commissioner's visit. The remains of the two French tourists on the beach were put into a mobile cold-storage unit awaiting transport back to Reykjavík. He paced, wringing his hands, awaiting the big boss's arrival.

The weather had shifted once again, with the rain and cloud lifting to allow the sun to blast the land with tranquil brightness. It really was a beautiful place beneath a summer-like glow. The sea glistened, while the southern lands bloomed with a lush green. Above all, though, was the magnificent Mýrdalsjökull glacier, its sheer breadth consuming the horizon. A stunning feature, completing a magnificent monolithic portrait of fire and ice. He went over the report one more time, just to be sure.

```
Lögreglan á höfuðborgarsvæðinu
INCIDENT REPORT
on behalf of the Ministry of the Interior


October 17th, 2017
```

THE BLACKENING

<u>Details of Incident:</u>
Female reported missing from Reynisfjara beach by boyfriend/travel companion. No trace found on inspection. Boyfriend, Ben Foster, arrested and detained in Vík for statement/further investigation.

The bodies of two unknown French tourists discovered on Reynisfjara beach. Mutilated remains. Nationality confirmed from shredded remains of passport among clothing. Names/Passport numbers - N/A.

<u>Details of Victims/Suspects/Missing Persons:</u>
Alison Carbery - 5' 8, brown hair, blue eyes. Nationality: UK
   (Missing)

2 x Unidentified French nationals. Both male, possible father and son. Remains.

(Suspect) Possibly at large. No lead/description.

Signed:
   Inspector   John   Ward
Varðstjóri, Vík
   John Ward

71

Commissioner Kári Ingason didn't hesitate in getting down to business, hauling Ingvar in to explain his findings. "I don't have time for this, Ingvar. This report is nothing but speculation. Tell me what happened here and why the hell Ward has this place on lockdown?"

Ingvar's verbal report was as bizarre as Ward's written one, and Kári struggled not to throw him out of the trailer. It was obvious that the lad was terrified being in front of him. After a bit of debate, the report was re-written. Satisfied with the changes, the curfew could now be lifted. He headed on foot towards The Grill – it was time to put this *buffoon* in his place.

Like something akin to an old western, the commissioner marched down the main road towards the Víkurskáli Grill, his swagger making it clear that he was angry and in search of answers beneath the midday sun.

Ward watched the red-faced figure approaching and decided to meet him head-on with diplomatic rationale. "Everything is in place, Sir. I've set a curfew, and Ingvar and I will monitor the homes and roads. If there is a killer around here, we'll find him."

Kári glared at him, the brooding silence adding to the tension. If Katla ever erupted, it would be nothing compared to the intensity in the man's eyes.

"Inspector, nice to see you again. Let me say this once and clearly..." He stepped forward until Ward could feel his hot breath on his face. "There will be no curfew or high-alert warning in this village."

"What? But, Sir, I don't think you—"

"—I understand just fine. I understand that the festival is going ahead tomorrow night and that you'll be a servant to this community, like you were sent here to be." Kári leaned back, his demeanour not calm, yet the way he looked down his nose was nothing short of condescending.

"But, Sir... have you read my report?"

His left cheek twitched. "Yes. Murder-suicide. How could a father do that to his own child? They are going back to Reykjavík now and the family will be notified when we confirm their identities." He shook his head and sighed. "Sadly, we are seeing more of this in our fine country these days."

Ward swallowed back an involuntary, whiskey-filled belch. "Sir, I don't think you understand what's happening here. We've two known dead, but there's also a girl miss—"

"I don't want to hear it, Inspector." He leaned in again, his nose twitching above a grimace. "You were warned not to cause trouble down here and, yet, here we are again. This is the second instance in a short space of time that I've been contacted over something you have done. The official report says the French man committed suicide after murdering his son."

"And what about Alison Carbery?" Ward countered, his tone sharper as he pushed to get through to this Icelandic dinosaur. What does the official report say about her? We can't ignore the fact that the woman is still missing."

"I read your report, and wondered why it was written so poorly. Perhaps the many rumours of your over-indulgences down here are true? Anyway, that's an issue for another day. A Search and Rescue squad is being prepared and will be dispatched as per normal procedure. You'll be wise not to challenge my handling of major situations under my jurisdiction, Inspector. Need I remind you that I know what you did back in Ireland? One more peep out of you and you'll be sent back badge-less on the first plane out of here."

Ward bit his tongue, not wanting Ingvar, or anyone else, knowing what happened in Dublin. He kept his mouth shut, his throat itching with a bitter lump of frustration. As he watched the commissioner speed away to the west of Vík, he knew Ingvar was shadowing him and had most likely overheard everything. He didn't have to say anything to the lad – his feelings were pretty clear: the commissioner had berated him, basically cut his authority from under him, and the only thought he had was to go and get it out of his mind. Ingvar stepped aside before he was pushed and Ward made a beeline for a drink.

"What about Ben Foster?" Ingvar called after him.

Ward stopped in his tracks. *Of course, Foster, the cheeky Belfast pup. Did he murder his girlfriend? I know by looking at him, the scrawny prick wouldn't have it in him.* As much as he wanted him to be guilty, especially because the case could be closed there and then, in his gut he knew the Northie was probably telling the truth. There was a time when he'd always relied on his hunches, before...

The bodies of the mutilated tourists stuck in his mind. Their families deserved answers. He ordered Ingvar back to the office. Time was running out, and the only person who could give them any answers was still handcuffed to the radiator.

EIGHT

Ward stood in front of Ben and stared him down. The young man was obviously still in shock, confused and scared. Despite his gut feeling, he reckoned the Northie knew more than he was letting on, but without proof it was impossible to know for sure. Forty-eight hours were up and he couldn't legally detain him any longer, so he was left with no option but to sign the release form and allow him leave the office.

Ingvar held the door open but Ben didn't move, other than getting to his feet and rubbing his raw wrist. "Hey, big man, what about my wee Ally?"

"The commissioner is dispatching the Search and Rescue team. If she's on this island, they'll find her." Ward sat at his desk, kneading his forehead with both hands, a drunken weariness creeping over him, so heavy he wasn't sure he could carry it any further. And despite the afternoon brightening up, he wondered how he still felt weary from the night before.

"Well, that's not good enough," Ben said. His voice didn't convey aggressive intent so Ward let it go. "Despite your bullish way about you, mate, I... I actually think you might be a decent bloke. When you sober up, maybe you can help me look for her?"

Ward looked up, his vision blurred from all the rubbing. "I'm no fucking good, boy. I can't protect anyone, let alone find someone missing on this fucked-up island. Good luck to you now."

"But—"

"Get out, lad, before I fuck you out."

Ben shook his head and left the office, but as he tried to exit, a man blocked the entrance – a mountain of a man, broad and husky – trying to regain his breath. Ward looked between Ingvar and Ben, who stood in silence as they watched the man drop a rucksack on the floor and make his way into the office, his hair and beard wild from the wind.

"Are you the Inspector dealing with the beach deaths and the missing woman?" he demanded in a booming voice.

"Who wants to know?" Ward asked, his words coming out hoarse. He struggled to keep his eyes open.

"I do, and if we are dealing with what I think we are dealing with, then you're going to need my help."

Ward looked at his cadet. "Ingvar, get these men out of here. I've had enough dealings with nutcases to do me for the next year."

"Hold on," Ben said, both arms out to his sides. "Shouldn't we hear what he has to say?"

"You two can fuck off out of here and talk about whatever you want to talk about. I'm in no mood." He eyed the drawer that held his whiskey. "Ingvar!"

The young man started ushering the men towards the door.

"Sir, my name is Rúnar Bergsson. I've travelled to Vík from the University of Iceland. It was not a short journey, I can assure you. I believe you are dealing with something here that will require my expertise."

Ward went to rest his head on his desk, but misjudged it and smacked it off the surface. "Fuck!"

He raised a hand. "Ingvar. I don't have time for this. Get them out of here!"

"Hold on, Sir." Ingvar said. "Mister Bergsson, are you connected with Ms Rakel—"

"Ingvar!"

"Yes, she is my colleague."

"Expertise in what, mate?" Ben asked.

Rúnar looked down at him. "I'm a biologist, but otherworldly delights and all the wonders that go with them interest me the most."

Ben's brows creased. "I'm sorry, mate, but what has that got to do with my Ally?"

"Ally? The missing girl, I assume?" Rúnar's broad shoulders slumped before he rose to his full height. "Ufology is a pastime of mine. And all the beautiful phenomena surrounding it."

Ben snorted more than laughed. "Flying saucers? Come off it, mate. You're talking bollocks."

"Science fiction and conspiracy theories?" Ingvar rested his hands on his narrow hips. "I didn't know they were subjects in the university."

Rúnar was a large man, with long scraggly hair and a greasy beard. Despite his massive appearance, Ward noticed that his eyes were small and beady. They narrowed at being mocked and everyone in the room was quick to notice his shoulders tense.

"Do not make jokes. Or else I'll put you through the wall. This is a very serious matter—"

"Hey!" Ward growled. "Don't you dare come in here and start throwing your weight around. I won't accept threats against my deputy. You may be a big man, but I'll fucking have you."

In the blink of an eye, Rúnar was leaning over the desk, butting heads with Ward, who had shot up and gave no quarter, even though his head felt fit to explode.

"Guys, what's with the aggression?" Ben shouted, getting between them. "Short fuses on the pair of ye. Cut this shit out. It's not going to find my Ally."

Ward didn't know how much longer he could keep it up, with the pressure on his neck close to unbearable. However, he wasn't going to back down from this overgrown geek. His taser was in the drawer... with his whiskey, but if he released his grip on the desk, he knew he'd end up on his arse.

His problem was solved when Ingvar somehow forced his way in from the other side, elbowing the pair apart with the help of Ben. Ward and Rúnar stepped back and glared at each other, the room silent except for their heaving breaths, steaming from the cold.

"What's this talk about little green men?" Ben asked, ending the non-verbal stand-off.

Ward looked from one to the other, picked up his jacket, and headed for the door. "Ingvar, I'm closing the station early. Show Foster out and send this tinfoil-hat-wearing loon on his way, too. You'll know where I'll be if you need me." He slammed the door shut behind him.

Rúnar turned to face Ben and Ingvar. "He's a drunk?"

Ingvar shrugged. "He's just working a few things out."

"What about my Ally," Ben asked.

The big man looked from one to the other. "What happened to her?"

"She is still missing," Ingvar said before Ben could respond.

Rúnar twisted his beard and nodded. "Hmm, it could be the return of Huldufólk." Ben frowned, his mouth open, while Ingvar rolled his eyes and turned away. "You know..." Rúnar said, "the Hidden People?"

"Okay, that's enough, Sir," Ingvar said, cutting the air with both hands. "We don't have time for myths and legends."

"Ha, I was joking. But if you want to treat me like a fool, then I'll show you the same respect."

Ingvar paled and looked down at the floor.

Rúnar groaned and shook his head, convinced he was wasting his time with these people. He needed to find whoever the real authority was in this place.

"But what has this got to do with my Ally? Are you saying she was taken by some sort of... alien?"

"No. I'm saying there are things in this world that go beyond human comprehension. And when these... things are disturbed, they can come into our world." He went on to tell them about the rats in the lab and how the test results could not be ignored. With the male rat being mutilated by the slime and the female becoming some sort of host for the entity, he figured this may be what was happening in Vík.

"What the...?" Ben's mouth hung open. "Are you saying that this sludge stuff has taken my Ally to... to fuck her?"

"Well, not exactly. I've read about this type of event before. I can explain more at the site of the incident. Can you show me where it is? Come, we are against the clock here." He ushered Ben towards the road.

"Hang on a minute, guys," Ingvar said. "You can't just go off tampering with a crime scene because you think some surreal conspiracy theory is a lead?"

"And what do you suggest?" Rúnar asked. *The police in this place were so unlikable.* "Wait until the inspector sobers up and hope he believes what is going on here?"

"If you say you're from the university, then I have to call Rakel."

"Call her, she'll verify everything. But I'm not waiting around."

"But—"

"Aye, sorry, mate, you signed me out and I need to find my Ally. Come on, Rúnar, man, let's get my equipment out of my car."

Rúnar grabbed up his rucksack and followed Ben out and down towards the beach. He glanced back to see the skinny cop watching the two of them. No time to wait for him to make his mind up. Storm clouds roiled over the horizon, as if sensing the impending dangers lurking beneath Vík. He urged Ben on, aware that something had changed in the air since his arrival. The place was so quiet. The silence, like the eye of a hurricane, lulling everyone into a false sense of security. Would they be ready for whatever was to come? Only time would tell, and he feared they didn't have much to play with.

NINE

Ben's mind was racing at a mile a second. According to Rúnar, fate and myth were the two forces that drove civilization towards completion. Fate was the understanding, while myths provided the knowledge of how everything came to pass and how they'd eventually end up coming to be. Together, they were hopelessly intertwined but, oddly, destined to work in parallel. Despite the big man's ramblings, he listened with intent. Something about his voice convinced him that he knew what he was talking about, even though his opinion on otherworldly forces seemed utterly outlandish, to say the least.

The mouth of the cave loomed and a light mist swirled around their calves as dusk crept in behind them. Thoughts of the unknown darkness ahead triggered fear deep in Ben's heart, but the hope of finding Alison alive and well pulled him forward.

"So, this is the place, yes?" Rúnar asked.

"Aye." He pointed at the exact spot Alison was attacked before being dragged off into the shadows. "She was right here, then in the next moment... gone."

Rúnar caressed his beard as he inspected the cavern, his gaze running over the ground and walls. "Whatever it was, it didn't leave much behind for us to track. We've no choice but to use our equipment and go in."

Ben took a moment to process the suggestion, after which he nodded. They had no other real option, especially with the local peelers seemingly unwilling and unable to do anything constructive. "Let's do it."

"Fear not, Ben, I have some experience navigating Icelandic cave networks. If she is in there, I believe we'll find her."

"I hope so." He fixed his hard hat and clicked the torch on before checking his gear, rented with the intention of hiking up a glacier with Alison in the hope of maybe finding the perfect moment to pop the question. Then he'd found this beach. If only they'd gone for the glacier or waited for the festival instead, things would have been so different.

He followed the big man into a tunnel, the light from their torches revealing wet walls and jagged icicles on the ceiling, each step creating monstrous shadows that loomed ahead before disappearing behind. Every now and then, he had to cough out the sulphuric sharpness of each breath, the sound echoing through the cave's intestines.

"Hey, mate, can we stop?" He hunkered down and took a swig from his water bottle. "We've been going for ages. I haven't eaten anything proper since I don't know when. I'm knackered."

Rúnar sat beside him in the narrow tunnel deep beneath the surface. "Ok, but only a few minutes. I don't want to stay down here longer than we have to."

A short time later they moved on, with Ben happy enough to follow the big man, glad to have someone with experience leading the way. The cave's network of passageways seemed never-ending, just waiting to swallow up the unwary in its cold and unforgiving bowels. The sulphuric air made his head spin, but he kept it to himself, not wanting to be a burden to this man who had so kindly offered his assistance in finding Ally.

Their descent felt steeper now and they'd made so many turns, he didn't know which way was which anymore.

"What are we doing, mate? Are we lost?" Even with their torches, the walls seemed darker and narrower, and the air felt heavier, harder to process.

"No, Ben, I do not believe so."

"How can you be sure? We haven't found any sign of Ally. We must have taken a wrong turn or something."

Rúnar released a long breath and massaged his beard, grimacing as he looked about them. "Leucauge Argyra."

"Huh? What was that, mate?"

Rúnar repeated the words and looked Ben in the eye. "It is the name of a spider that becomes host to a wasp. I have reason to believe, after hearing your account of the incident, that the fate of that creepy crawly and the missing girl are... how do you say? Similar."

"I'm sorry, mate, what? Please drop the cryptic speech and spell this shit out for me."

"It is an advanced form of evolution which I have studied in great detail. The spider spins big webs to catch its prey. Think of humans working the same way when building cities. But there is a parasite, and no matter how advanced we become or our technical achievements, we are still just meat and bones beneath it all, and if we become infected, we go back to year zero, or worse – wiped out entirely."

Ben took his helmet off, rubbed his head and dropped his torch, the light creating dancing shadows around them. "How do you know all this?"

"I pay close attention to the details, especially stuff that is confidential on the internet." He laughed before pointing to markings along the tunnel's floor – black, crusty bits, like ash, which reminded Ben of burnt pieces of toast. "See, that is not normal for the inside of this cave. I've been following it, just like I've been following a woman who was dragged off into the dark by some sort of 'shadowy oil'."

Ben got to his feet and examined the weird lumps dotting the stone floor. "What are they?"

"Deposits from someone or something that made its way through this tunnel shortly before us." Rúnar's eyes narrowed as he focused further down the tunnel. "I found this earlier." He held up a piece of torn clothing.

Ben's breath caught and he had to cough it out. "That's... Ally's!" He spat a wad of phlegm behind. "What the fuck, mate?"

"I had to be sure before telling you."

"About what? That you found a clue and kept walking without saying anything? That's fucked up." His voice bounced off the tunnel walls.

"Okay, take it easy for a second. Let me explain—"

Ben squared his shoulders as he glared up at the bearded Icelandic. "You've got five seconds before I start swinging, mate."

Rúnar took off his hard hat and remained silent for a long moment, his features flat under the light of Ben's head torch. "Okay. You said that something black and slimy came from the cave? It moved towards your lady friend and appeared to be conscious before attacking her and dragging her down here. Correct?"

"Yeah, that's pretty much it," Ben said, taking a step back, realising how close he'd come to trying to tackle this giant of a man.

"Okay, I don't think this was the work of some mere animal. Something about this whole thing doesn't make sense, which I'm sure you agree, yes? I need to find the girl's body so—"

"Alison. Her name is Alison!"

"Okay. My apologies. Alison. I need to find her one way or another so I can be sure. I believe something otherworldly is at work here."

Ben let out a loud sigh. *Not this shit again. Maybe Ward was right, maybe there is a killer on the loose and this bloke knows more than he's letting on? Ufology? Bollocks. For all I know, Alison's killer could be standing in front of me, having led me into a death-*

trap. The lads back home used to say his gullible side would get him into trouble someday. Maybe that day had arrived. It wouldn't be difficult for a person to go missing this deep beneath the surface and never be seen again.

The big man kept talking, droning on, his voice bouncing off the walls. "Please, stop. Just stop. You said you wanted to help. We don't even know where we are."

"I am helping," Rúnar said. He shook his head, put his hat back on, and walked down the tunnel. "I was only trying to prepare you for what you're about to see."

The passageway veered almost at a right angle to their left and took them into a large clearing, the ceiling a perfect dome. Water trickled from the wall on the far side, rising steam indicating its thermal properties. But that wasn't what concerned either of them as they laid eyes on what lay on the floor across the cavern.

"Ally!"

Ben ran over, his knees crashing against the stone floor as he slid up beside her. She looked like an angel, her skin perfect, the hair on her head vibrant and flowing. As he held her in his arms, he could have sworn he heard music play in the background, setting the mood for a lovers' embrace – warm, caring – her voice singing their favourite song to him, signalling their reunification and lifting his heart in rapture.

"I love you," he declared, his love for her bringing tears of joy.

Then a large hand tugged at his shoulder. "Ben..."

He shook it off, pulling his darling closer.

"Ben..."

Rúnar's grip tightened, digging into him to such an extent that he had no choice but to turn, and that's when he realised that the place in which he knelt was not as it seemed. The water that flowed from the wall was nothing more than a stain, an ancient scrape that bore no resemblance to the steaming font he's seen. A trick of the mind. A horrible dread filled him as the beam from his headlamp darted from wall to ceiling and back again.

Nothing. Bleak, stinking nothing.

The cavern spun, and he prayed that some toxic emission played a part in warping his perception. But that wasn't the case. The love of his life lay heavy and cold in his arms, like a stone. He gripped her shoulders so he could gaze upon her face. An ice-cold horror ran through him and he broke into tears at the sight of what lay before him. "Ally? No!"

Her face, lifeless and pale – her hands and feet, only moments ago pristine, were now decayed like volcanic ash. Bile filled his mouth as he looked at her hair – matted and rotting, like wizened straw in random patches along her scalp, and her stomach, so bloated, as if ready to pop. Everything about her reeked of human corruption – even her once-beautiful eyes, which now bulged like two large black bubbles staring back at him.

He hugged her to him, trembling as he begged her to wake up. "No, Ally, no. What happened to you? Who did this to you? Talk to me, please! Baby! Darling, please!"

An arm came around his shoulders. "Ben... Come, let's get her out."

"Rúnar?" He looked up at the bearded scientist. "Please, mate, I don't know what to do here. Help her. I know you know something. Please!" He trailed off as sobs wracked his body. "I'm so sorry, baby. I'm so, so sorry."

The big Icelandic eased him away from Alison's body. He then searched for a pulse, resting two fingers at the side of her neck. Then his brows knitted, possibly in confusion, or maybe disbelief.

"Ben... We have to get her to the medical centre. She... she is not dead." He pulled a penknife from his bag and set about cutting her loose from the tendrils of sludge that held her firm against the cavern floor. The slime reacted as if in pain, slithering and pulsating, finally redrawing between cracks in the ground.

"We have to get her out of here. This place is alive."

TEN

Ingvar Berg always followed the rules. Even from a young age, he favoured regulations and structure instead of testing boundaries, and always respected his peers and superiors. This outlook gave him a level of maturity that went far beyond his years, so when he saw Ward continue down his path of destruction, he felt like he was the only one in the world who cared enough to try and help him. With daylight gone, it was no surprise that he found him at the Grill and pulled up a stool beside him.

Ward refused to acknowledge his presence for the guts of an hour, but this didn't deter Ingvar from reaching out to let him know that someone on this island actually gave enough of a shit to care about him, no matter how stubborn he acted.

"You're wasting your time, boy," Ward eventually spat out. "Why don't you just head on home and leave me be?"

"The only one wasting their time is you," Ingvar said. "The drink won't save you, John. Only you can save yourself."

"Don't preach to me. I know I'm no good." He knocked back a mouthful of Flóki. "The world doesn't need more losers like me in it."

Ingvar wanted to slap him with all he could muster but, instead, he drew a deep breath and told the story of how his father was never there for him. It took some telling, but evoked no reaction, as if the words went in one ear and straight out the other.

He stifled a frustrated groan. "Well, if you're not interested in my past, Chief, then why don't you indulge me in yours?"

"What you mean, boy?" Ward slurred, his eyes half-closed under the weight of too many single malts.

Ingvar took a moment to smell his beer and let the froth fizzle against his nose. "You know what I mean, John. What the hell is an Irishman doing all the way up here in Vík, anyway?" He swallowed a ball of tension. "You're running from something, aren't you?"

"Nnno."

"Well then, why are you here? You don't seem to give a shit about anyone or anything here, other than drinking yourself into a grave."

"It's none of your business, boy. Drop it."

"No. Not until you open up. I may only be the deputy, but I'm also your partner. That means I've got your back. But I can't help you if you hide in the bottom of that whiskey glass."

Ward snorted and snotted as he exhaled through his nostrils, forcing looks of disgust from other customers. He wiped his mouth and chin on his sleeve, cleared his throat, then proceeded to tell the story of how he ended up on his secondment. His home was burgled a few years ago by a bunch of thugs he knew from the council estates back home. *Scum of the Earth* is the term he used to describe them. But that wasn't the reason he had to leave. The trauma from what had happened never went away and he took to the bottle to help mask it.

Which was fine for a while... but one hot summer's afternoon, he was doing a routine raid on a house – *a bust*. The job was a success and they got what they needed to put the local criminal operation out of business. But during his final walk of the premises, he heard a noise coming from one of the upstairs wardrobes. Inside was a young lad, scared and begging not to be hurt. At first, Ward planned just to rough him up a bit and maybe send him home with few bruises and a stern warning. However, when he got a good look at the lad's face, memories of the robbery came flooding back. At first, he recalled the horrific expressions of his wife and daughter, Fiona and Niamh – the look of fear still haunted him to this day. But that feeling soon morphed into rage, and before he knew what he was doing, his partner at the time was pulling him off the youth. Ward's knuckles were burst, oozing blood – almost showing bone. On the floor, the teen, twitching and looking like he'd just be mauled by a pack of savage dogs.

The attending medic advised Ward to watch out for an overwhelming feeling of remorse later on, but Ward picked bits of teeth from beneath the cuts on his knuckles and just nodded as he politely told him to 'fuck off'.

His superiors were informed, and because the boy turned out to be the son of a *somebody* – a government minister – it went right to the top. The Garda Commissioner called to Ward's home and offered him a chance to relocate: '*A few years to lay low and get yourself straight.*'

Ward didn't have much choice in the matter, and before he knew what was happening, he found himself flying over the north Atlantic to the land of fire and ice.

"I'm sorry to hear this, Chief," Ingvar said, placing a hand on his shoulder. "At least you ended up here."

Ward shrugged it off. "I'm done, Ingvar. I can never go home. There's nothing there for me anymore."

"What about your family?"

"What family?"

Ingvar finally gave up, deciding he was done for the night – the story was a lot to take on, and he felt unable to take on anymore troubles until he had time to process everything. Ward was a hardened man, but he never had him down for a violent person, and with that he finished his drink and left his chief in his sullen, drunken state at the bar. All he could hope was the man would be okay in the morning.

Ward woke to the sound of his door being banged near off its hinges. Someone on the other side was calling his name. He struggled to gain control of his thoughts, blinking away the haze as the room spun.

Whoever was outside sounded impatient, and he felt sure it was a woman. *What the fuck is wrong now?*

He had enough to deal with as it stood, with everything in Vík falling around him – the last thing he wanted was another crisis added to his list. After rolling out of bed and struggling to get yesterday's pants and vest on, he stumbled over to the door. "I'm coming! Hold your fucking horses."

His reflection in the mirror almost frightened him. He ruffled his hair, then unchained the door and inched it open.

"John, I—"

"What the fuck are you doing here?" he barked at a flustered Rakel.

"I've been looking for you all over town."

"For what? Haven't you heard? This town cares more about making money than the safety of the public."

"Yeah, Ingvar told me. Can I come in?"

He looked over his shoulder. His place could only be described as a pigsty. In fact, he considered that disingenuous to the animal. No, he was actually living in squalor. A rush of shame washed over him, "Sure, but, it's a bit of mess."

Rakel pushed past him, seemingly unphased by the empty beer bottles and overflowing ashtrays, along with the stale tobacco stench that permeated the space. "I see you like to keep healthy."

Ward shrugged and remained by the door, allowing her time to get to whatever she'd come for.

She looked him up and down, then coughed into her hand, as if she'd breathed in too much for her liking. "What happened with the meeting?" she asked, stepping into the centre of the room. "Why isn't the town on alert?"

Ward closed his eyes and sighed, but everything spun so he opened them and tried to focus on her. "Money. It's all about fucking money."

She pushed him for an explanation, and he told her that the committee wanted to keep talk of alerts and killers under wraps until the Festival of Lights had concluded. The decision hadn't sat well with him – not one bit – and the meeting ended with a violent outburst and swift exit.

"What happens now?" she asked, her features softening.

Ward didn't like the idea that she might be taking pity on him. The last thing he wanted was her sympathy, though it wasn't such a bad thing that she'd lost her angsty demeanour. He stepped across the room, aware that she was watching his every move. Something about her, the way she stood – how she watched him – told him that she was involved in her own inner struggle. *Two tormented souls in the middle of nowhere...*

"I asked—"

"I heard you," he snapped, opening the window blind. Her thin shoulders slumped and he regretted his terse response. He had no answer for her. All he had was drink. *What the fuck else is left?* He ran both hands through his hair, raking his nails across his scalp.

"People have died, John. You have to keep fighting."

"No, I'm done. Just leave me be..."

Before he knew it, her hands were on his shoulders and she'd pulled him around to face him, her eyes locking with his. A moment passed, stretched out to what felt like an eternity as he was drawn, like a magnet, into the depths of her pain. The floorboards moaned from their weight slapping down on them. He found himself on top, her nails scraping along his back as he unzipped her jacket. She clung to him - ground into him - as if in desperation. He took charge, easing away to get to her pants, but she retained their connection with her soft lips and probing tongue, ushering him on with gentle murmurs that drove him into a fever.

She kept eye contact as he positioned himself, her intense gaze somewhat disconcerting, but he was ready, and wet his cock with spit before ramming it into her.

The floorboards squealed and squeaked as he pounded her, and when he had to ease off to catch his breath, she gripped him between her legs and urged him on, loving it, rocking and bucking beneath him, climbing towards her climax. He tried to match her, tried to force the visions away as she braced herself, nuzzling her forehead against his shoulder, encouraging him – egging him on – bringing him with her as she arched her back and tensed up. But he couldn't banish the faces, the eyes – the heartbreak.

He stopped, gasping as he stared down at her. *Rakel?* He looked around the room, his head pounding, then got off her and backtracked to the door. Her vision focused, and she stared at him, her gaze moving to his limp cock, then up to the tears running down his cheeks.

"What the fuck?" she blurted. "Why'd you stop?"

"I'm sorry. This happens, sometimes. The booze or something..." He covered his face with both hands as despair surged through him, but he couldn't prevent a howling sob from escaping. *What the fuck?*

"It's okay," she whispered, her touch soft on the back of his hand. "It's okay. It happened to my ex a few times..."

He didn't look at her, just lowered his head, his shoulders shaking, and waited for her to hold him, even though a part of him wanted to fight her off, to fight everyone off. As they embraced, holding each other in the silence, it occurred to him that they may both be trying to escape from their own demons, their paths crossing here in one of the remotest places on Earth, possibly bringing a sense of hope, if there was any left in the world?

He apologised again, got himself dressed and cleaned up and waited by the door for her. Without speaking, he showed her the way to the Toyota. He could sense her disappointment and, by way of peace, offered her a drink. And as expected, she declined with a scoff before climbing into the vehicle. She reached down in the passenger foot well and pulled up a weather-beaten camera and tripod. "What's this?"

"Oh, I forgot about that," Ward answered, pulling his door closed. "Found it outside the cave the other night."

"Are you serious, John? You found a camera at a possible murder scene and forgot about it?"

"Er... I was drunk–"

"You're always drunk, John! You need to get a grip. People depend on you."

They both sat in silence for a few moments. He sensed her frustration and decided against arguing further, turning the ignition before heading for the station.

"She's alive!" Rakel shouted after feeling the cold woman's pulse. A palpable sense of relief permeated the room – none more than Ben, who cried while repeatedly kissing Alison's forehead.

Rakel looked at Rúnar and Ingvar, who stood sheepishly at the back of the room. And then to Ward, who had slumped at the news, and who now stared down at the other Irishman, a pained expression on his face.

He blinked and met her gaze. "How could I have been so wrong? If it wasn't... I don't know. What exactly are we dealing with here?" He let out a frustrated sigh and examined the busted camera. With a click, he removed the SD card, moved across the room and handed it to Rúnar. "I found the camera in front of the cave..."

He took one last look around the room, gave Rakel a nod that she understood as: *do your best*, then left.

A part of her wanted to follow him. She worried for him. Who knew what he was capable of in such a vulnerable state? Still, her job was here with the girl. "We have to get her airlifted to Landspítali University hospital in Reykjavík."

Her suggestion was met with silence.

"She's right," Ingvar said.

"There is nothing more I can do for her here. She is in some sort of coma and needs a specialist."

"Okay, love," Ben said, sighing with resignation, "let's get her out of here."

They spent the next few minutes preparing her for transportation. But something didn't seem right – her eyes shone with a jet-black gleam, almost pulsating under the cabin lights. Her teeth and fingernails had the same gleam, and with a noticeable boost in length.

Rakel walked out to the cabin's porch and took a moment to process everything before making the emergency call. After witnessing what she had in the lab, she knew something wasn't right. She took in the sea view for a few moments. Something deep inside compelled her not to press dial, because if she did, then the girl might never be seen again.

The view was stunning, with dark roiling clouds looming in the distance and wild waves crashing against the stacks in their efforts to reach the shore.

She was pulled back to the moment when Rúnar blocked her light. The big man was flustered, full of purpose. He stopped for a second, gave her a concerned look, then headed back inside and set himself up at Ward's desk, removing a laptop from his bag.

The midday sun was hidden behind overcast clouds from the south. A whistling breeze could be heard outside, signalling a bout of bad weather.

Rúnar tapped and clicked away furiously on his keyboard, then stopped with a gasp. He cleared his throat, as if about to deliver a presentation to a large forum. "I think I know what is going on." He glanced at Rakel, then took in Ben and the unconscious Alison. "We are dealing with a serious situation here, and I believe that whatever is happening to Alison – the stuff in the lab, the inside of the cave – it's all connected. There is something... evil lurking beneath this village." He looked to the ceiling.

"What are you talking about, mate?" Ben asked, his face scrunched up.

"Hold on, Mister Foster," Ingvar said. "Let him speak. What did you find?"

"I'm talking about a threat to everyone on this island. Hold on..."

Rakel held her breath as he proceeded to tap keys and scroll, the light from the screen shifting and changing on his face as he worked. Then he sat back, staring at whatever lay in front of him.

"Rúnar?"

He looked at her, then stood and turned the laptop around to show the room.

"What the?" Ingvar blurted out in shock at images of the French boy, suspended from the roof of the cave by what appeared to be black tendrils, horror etched across his face.

"My God," Rakel exclaimed, covering her mouth with her hand.

"I know, right?" Rúnar agreed. "This is no man or animal."

Ben snorted. "What, like, E fucking T?"

"Who knows? Perhaps it is more like a parasite."

"A what?" Ingvar asked.

"Think about it. What gender where the French tourists?"

"Both male."

"Yes, and both destroyed. But not Alison. I'm assuming Alison is a female, right?"

"Last time I checked, mate."

"Okay, so putting that together with what happened with the rats in the lab... I think whatever the creature is in these pictures, it wants to eliminate the threat of a male, while using a female as a host."

"You're saying my Ally is pregnant?"

"More like... invaded. She is alive in her body, but something else is in there with her."

Ben blinked a rapid sequence. "What, like... possessed?" He looked down at Alison, then back at the big man, his mouth hanging open. "Are you saying my Ally is fucking possessed? Call the fucking exorcist, mate."

Rakel stepped forward. "Yes, Rúnar, what are you suggesting?"

"If only it were so simple. No, I'm saying we go into the cave and find the source of whatever it is. Then we kill it. Otherwise there is no hope for your Alison."

His suggestion was met with silence.

"Kill it?" Ben held both hands out, palms up. "With what?"

"I can get some explosives," Rúnar answered, straightening to his full height.

"Of course, you can," Rakel said, rolling her eyes. *Where is the inspector when we need him?*

The four of them deliberated the issue, eventually coming to the conclusion that perhaps Rúnar was right. After the strange occurrences of the last few days, he might be on to something. First Alison went missing, dragged away by black sludge, only to be found in a coma-like state, with those dark eyes. Then the bodies on the beach – or the remnants of bodies. No, this was not the work of a serial killer, like Ward had assumed – this was the doing of something more sinister, possibly more dangerous than any man, and unless they found out exactly what lay in the depths of the cave, the fate of everyone on the island could be in serious jeopardy. But they couldn't do it without John Ward.

ELEVEN

What the fuck is wrong with me? I can't even get it up anymore. Oh, Fiona, wherever you are, I am sorry for everything. I tried to save our Niamh – I really did. I did everything in my power to save her. And us... But I failed. Just like I'm failing to save Alison and this shit-splat village in the middle of fucking nowhere.

As he sat in the Toyota, overlooking the sea, Ward was sure he'd reached his breaking point. *It's time to go.* His past, this present, were all too much, and as he wrapped his drunken lips around the barrel of his gun, he felt like everything would soon to be okay. *Just pull the trigger, man. Squeeze the bastard and put an end to it all.*

He clenched his eyes shut and bit down on the barrel, but it was no good, he couldn't do it. As much as he convinced himself over and over that this was what he really wanted, he could never do it. The bullet never left the chamber. He pulled the weapon out of his mouth.

"Fuck!"

He re-holstered it and took a slug of whiskey, which burned the throat off him and brought on a bout of coughing that had him gagging and retching into the passenger foot-well.

The weather had turned for the worse, with a heavy rain sweeping in from the sea, drenching the village. Dark, overcast clouds made telling the time of day difficult, but he didn't care. *What does the time matter when today isn't the day I'll die?* Instead, he headed for his office. Soon, the village would be overrun with tourists. The festival was going ahead regardless of the weather, it wasn't an issue for Icelanders, who loved the old saying: *If you don't like the weather, just wait fifteen minutes.*

His appearance in the doorway interrupted a busy conversation between Ingvar, Rakel, Ben, and Rúnar. Long stares accompanied their silence.

"Chief, you're back!" Ingvar said, clearly delighted. He glanced at the others, then raised his brows at Ward. "Glad you decided to join us, Sir."

"What's the occasion?"

"Rúnar has something to tell you."

Ward steadied himself against the door frame. This was one of the rare times when he admitted to himself that he'd drank too much, probably to the point where he was only fit for bed. In the back of his mind, he convinced himself that his liver had given up. But he held it together and listened to the big man's theory: the slime; the deaths; Alison. As soon as he heard her name, his focus sparked and he couldn't take his eyes off her – the still body, inhabited by something none of them could really explain. And as much as Rúnar tried to convince him, a part of him held on to the hope that this was nothing more than the work of some man or a bad dream. But when he was shown the pictures from the cave, he agreed that an investigative probe was a good idea. Even being full of drink, he felt good at the prospect of doing some proactive police work.

Then the reality hit him. *Shit!* "I've to make a call."

"To who?" Rakel asked.

If it were anyone else, he would have told them to mind their own fucking business. But not her.

"Kári..."

"John, really?" Ingvar said. "After the last time?"

"This village is in trouble, kid. The last thing we need is for it to be overrun with drunk tourists, with nothing better to do than take Instagram pictures and hash-tagging to the world about what's going on here."

"Bit of a leap there, Chief."

"Maybe. Perhaps we should let them arrive and get slaughtered by whatever the fuck is lurking in that cave?"

"Man's got a point," Rakel said.

Ward took his phone out. "We need to cancel the festival. Now."

"Sir, I don't think you understand the situation we are dealing with here." Ward squeezed his mobile, but it was no use – the slightest hint of putting the town on alert was enough to set Kári off. And the tirade from the end of the line had his ear burning.

"Listen to me, Ward. If you tell that committee anything other than the village is safe and ready to host the festival, I'll have your head on a plate. It's too important to the economy. Damn it, man, we can sort all this out once the weekend is over and the crowds have gone."

"At the cost of lives?"

"Save the hysteria for drunken bar stories, Ward. Now, be a good boy and do as you're told. I'll be there in about two hours and everything had better be in order."

Ward admitted defeat. He couldn't muster the energy to take the commissioner on. Not after the last few days. Once the call ended, he returned to the room and shrugged. "I give up. To hell with this place. Fuck it all." Then he left.

Ingvar followed him out to the 4x4. "Chief, where are you going?"

"A long way from here, kid. This place doesn't need a bitter old drunk like me."

"But, Chief, we need you. Please!"

"Forget it. I'm done. Tell the committee that the festival is on and everything is okay." He shook his head and rolled up the jeep's window.

As he drove down the road, he passed the first wave of incoming rental cars. The clouds had parted to allow the stars to shine, and soon the lights would be on show and thousands would gather to appreciate them. He gripped the steering wheel with both hands, hoping the festival would pass without incident, but his well-tested police instincts knew that wouldn't be the case.

TWELVE

The Festival of Lights, now in full swing, had attracted thousands of tourists to Vík's black-sand beach. Everyone was in a great mood, their wonder buoyed by some of life's enhancers: beer, weed, and other mind-alternating substances. The rain clouds had moved on and even though he was no stranger to the northern lights, Ingvar was still mesmerized by the waves dancing across the heavens, all shades of green with flicks of purple, elegantly painting the sky as revellers rejoiced at one of the most mesmerizing phenomena the world had to offer.

Commissioner Kári, overlooking the spectacle, had instructed the additional police officers to take up vantage points around the crowd. Ingvar was convinced that Ward's warning had forced him to take extra precautions. Thankfully, though, the incidents over the last few days hadn't gone viral to the wider world, especially with the tourists busy basking in the light extravaganza.

"Commissioner, the men are all in place," he said, "and everything has gone to plan so far."

"Good." Kári barely acknowledged him. "Make sure the revellers are contained on the beach. I don't want the village overrun with drunks and stoners."

"Yes, Sir." As Ingvar followed his orders, assisting with the crowd control, he couldn't help but find the whole thing beautiful. The village was vibrant and alive, filled with happy people experiencing pure joy. *I wish the chief was here to see this.* Then he looked above the beach and noticed a 4x4 speeding towards the village. *The chief?* A part of him wanted to jump with relief, while the other feared what another encounter with Kári would do to him. Ward wasn't in the right state of mind – angry, resentful, and no doubt suffering the effects of a hard night's drinking, which would add fuel to the brewing tensions. *I'd better get back.* He broke into a sprint.

The Toyota skidded to a halt in front of Kári. Ward emerged, a bag on his shoulder, his hair tossed, eyes tired and dark. Ingvar figured he was drunk, and Kári must have too, because he looked him up and down with disgust.

"You're a disgrace to the badge, Ward."

He didn't reply, looking instead at Ingvar, who gasped as he tried to catch his breath from the run. "These people are in danger."

"Not another word from you," Kári barked. "You're a drunk." He turned to Ingvar. "Take the jeep back to the office. Then return here and assist Inspector Ward with his crowd-control duties. It will be his last time wearing the badge on this island."

Ward glared, his eyes bulging as he approached the commissioner, and Ingvar feared he was going to attack the man. His frown was so deep, it was obvious that he was fighting an inner battle, probably an urge to unleash a flurry of punches at their commander. If the chief was right, they had a bigger battle on their hands, and if he attacked Kári, then they had already lost.

The chief bit his lower lip and let out a long breath that had Ingvar sighing with relief – cut short by a piercing scream from down on the beach.

"What was that?" Kári snapped, looking around.

"We're too late," Ward said, shaking his head.

A wave of panic washed over the crowd as the lights continued dancing in the night sky. At first, the screams came from near the mouth of the cave, then from the other end of the beach, and before they knew it, a full-scale act of terror was unfolding. In every direction, something was happening, with tourists, police officers, and locals all overcome with confusion and fear. Slime oozed at a rapid rate from the cave, spilling out onto the beach. It moved so fast, attacking at a ferocious pace, that people had no time to escape. Some were pulled to the sand and dragged back into the darkness, while others were mutilated in front of their terrified loved ones.

Ward raced along the beach, screaming at the top of his lungs for everyone to head back to the village, but it was futile. Nearly every person he passed was already dead or wounded. Before he knew it, he was surrounded by limbs. And as he stopped to examine what looked like a child's arm, slime emerged from beneath the sand, like a tentacle, and snatched at the loose body part. He tried beating the sludge off, but it only dissolved and receded for a moment before reforming and swiping at him, knocking him to the sand. Items clinked in his bag. He unzipped it and rifled through its contents, but the slime was so fast, wrapping around his leg, and before he knew it, he was being pulled along the sand at pace, just about managing to hold onto the bag. People around him were a blur and he lost sense of direction, even up and down, until he saw the mouth of the cave. With a roar, he grabbed at anything, eventually catching the leg of a man – the hairy barman from The Grill – bringing him down, his added weight forcing the slime to a stop.

"Let go of me," the guy screamed, his eyes wide with stupefied terror. "Get off. Get off!"

Ward wanted to respond but, before he could, the sludge shot forward, caught hold, and the man was whipped away. His screams echoed through his head, and when he sat up, all he could do was watch as the barman was torn to bits at the mouth of the cave, along with so many others.

The blood-soaked sand around him rose and bubbled. *Fuck! This thing isn't going to stop.* Then he realized the slime was still on his leg. He rummaged in his bag and pulled out a knife and a can of antifreeze, remembering what Rakel had said about the thing's reaction to cold. Pain shot up both his legs, and bile rose into his mouth as the slime's grip tightened and it started dragging him beneath the black sand, not over it. He roared as he struggled to free himself, slashing at the slime with the knife, but the cuts had no discernible effect. As the tentacle climbed up and wrapped itself around his torso, he knew he was seconds away from disappearing under the sand, maybe into the bowels of the mountain, and vanishing without a trace.

He tried to breathe as the sludge's grip tightened around his chest. *I'm fucked!* Then it stopped and lifted him, and he assumed it was preparing to whip him under. *No way!* He sprayed the thing full-on with the antifreeze, causing an instant reaction. The slime recoiled and its grip loosened, as if confused about this unexpected attack. *A weakness. Rakel was right.*

Without delay, he directed the spray across the top of the sludge, evoking an ear-piercing screech as it contracted and released him from its death grip. He scrambled to his feet and backtracked a few metres. The antifreeze had momentarily shocked the sludge into an inactive state. *Without an ocean of this shit, there's no way I can stop this horror.*

"Chief, help me! Help!" a young man called from the dark, his words etched with panic. Ward darted over bloodied body parts to see Ingvar in a struggle with the black slime. When he reached the cadet, more slime burst from the sand in the shape of two large tentacles. They slapped against each other, like a butcher preparing a pig for slaughter, with Ingvar held helpless in front of them. Ward saw that the young lad's legs had been severed, and with every word he tried to speak, blood gurgled from his mouth.

"Ingvar!" He tried to attract the slime's attention but it was only interested in one thing. The tentacles swooped down and wrapped themselves around his cadet's torso, the brutal move forcing a stream of dark blood from the young man's gaping mouth. Ward grabbed hold of Ingvar's arms and engaged in a tug-of-war. He dug his feet into the sand, using every ounce of his strength to hold on. Moments later, after the most-horrific popping sound, he found himself on his back with Ingvar lying on top of him. He pushed himself out from beneath him and rolled up onto his knees. All around him, screaming and crying people were dragged past, into the mouth of darkness. The sand rumbled, bubbling as more slimy tentacles emerged. Everything spun as he tried to get a grip on the nightmare, then, as if someone had flicked a switch, the screams faded as the beach emptied.

An eerie silence descended against the gentle backdrop of lapping surf. When he looked around, all that was left were bloodied body parts and the drag marks of those who'd screamed their way into the darkness.

As he struggled to control his breathing, he couldn't help but notice the swirling colours in the sky, dancing effortlessly above the horror. He wished for an escape, but was distracted by Ingvar's cold hand gripping his wrist.

His instinct was to tell the lad things would be all right, but the sight before him told him it would be a waste of time. The boy lay on the sand, his body severed from mid-torso down – a bloodied mess – organs free from beneath the rib cage, soaking in a pool of blood. His gaze, filled with fear as it fixed on Ward, begging him to save him, but all Ward could do was comfort him while he listened to his final, bloodied breath releasing into the dancing night sky.

THIRTEEN

No number of words could describe Ward's anger as he stormed towards the police cabin, the rage consuming him like an eruption from Katla. The same thoughts kept repeating over and over in his head: *It's all your fault, Kári, you fucking prick! How could you let this happen? And for what? Money? Was it really worth it?*

Beneath his fury, a deep sadness pained his heart. He'd been fond of the boy, even though he always gave him a hard time. That was only because he saw potential in him, and wanted nothing but the best for him. He deserved better, and so did the village.

Warlike scenes surrounded him beneath the glowing night sky. Bodies torn to pieces – the rank smell of death mixing with the sea breeze. And despite witnessing the slime unleash its horror, he still found it hard to fully comprehend what could have done such a terrible thing. Whatever it was, it was alive – coordinated and cunning – with all the traits of an experienced predator. It knew what it wanted and nothing could get in its way. Well, almost nothing – the anti-freeze repelled it, but the village would need a tanker of the stuff if they hoped to fatally injure the viscous blob.

As he approached the steps to the cabin, he noticed the door was ajar. A trail of blood drops stained the decking leading towards the road west. Ward stormed in, his Glock drawn, and was stunned at the sight before him. Ben was facedown and motionless on the floor. The office was trashed, his desk upended, papers scattered about, with blood sprayed across the walls.

Ben groaned and twitched.

He's alive!

Ward rushed to his aid and turned him on his back. The young man's eyes were glazed and distant.

"Foster. Are you alright? Talk to me, lad."

"Where… where is she?"

Ward looked around. "Who?"

"Ally?"

"You're here on your own, lad. What happened?"

Ben struggled to sit up, coughing and spitting, barely able to catch his breath. "When… I heard shit kicking off down on the beach, she… came alive, mate. Her eyes… so black. It was the scariest thing I've ever seen." He coughed and spat again. "It wasn't my Ally."

"What happened next?"

"She stood up, all tense, then vomited blood and some of that black stuff. I tried to calm her down, but she picked me up and slammed me against the wall."

"She's half your size, Ben. How'd—"

"That stuff. It's in her." He wiped blood from his brow, smearing his forearm. "It's doing things to her. She was… I don't know. I think it controlled her and she took off away. I wanted to follow, but everything spun and I must have passed out."

Ward surveyed the room. Apart from the mess, nothing suggested that the northerner was lying. After all he'd seen and experienced down on the beach, what happened here was plausible. *The slime. Where did it come from? How long as it been lurking beneath the Earth?* He looked at his gun before holstering it. *How the fuck am I going to kill it?*

He led Ben outside to get some fresh air. On the decking by the door, he noticed a crinkled-up photograph. When he picked it up, he was hit with a rush of sadness. Alison and Ben, hugging in what had to be happier times. Her smile pained his heart, reminding him of his daughter. Everything about her reminded him of his little Niamh – the hair, eyes and teeth – a striking resemblance to the apple of his eye.

His mind cast back to the night his house was invaded, the painful memories still as fresh as the day they were formed. The terror on his daughter's face moments before she was taken would forever haunt him. And the sinister laugh from the masked man who pulled the trigger would ring in his ears until the day he died. How could anyone recover from that? He considered himself the *man of the house* – the protector of his girls – the breadwinner, with all that goes with the role. *I failed them. I was supposed to protect them and I didn't. I could have done more... I should have!*

If only she'd listened to her mother. For weeks before that fateful night, Fiona had implored Niamh to move out. After all, she was twenty-three and had landed a good job straight from college. He'd sat back and let her do all the nagging. If only he'd taken the lead, Niamh wouldn't have been in the house that night, and more importantly, she'd still be alive.

He didn't blame Fiona for leaving him, and although he needed his rock during a time of overwhelming grief, he'd resigned himself to the fact that she wanted to be away from him, needing to make a fresh start elsewhere. How could he hold that against her?

Like him, she'd witnessed their daughter's execution, in what the papers called a *Gangland-style Revenge Murder*. And for what? For doing his job? For doing the right thing? For being the stand-up guy in the community, who wasn't afraid to tackle the dealers and degenerates? It broke his heart, and was all for nothing. Or was it? He didn't see himself as a particularly religious man – unlike most his age back home. Things like that were only mentioned out loud when it suited.

The breeze lifted the photo and he caught it with his thumb. He traced Alison's head with his nail. *Perhaps I'm supposed to save this girl? But how can I do that when everyone I care about ends up dead? Please, God, give me a sign.*

Kári appeared, as if out of nowhere, striding towards the cabin, flustered and agitated. He powered past

Ward and Ben, into the room, and slapped the upended table. "Where's the dammed phone?"

"You son of a bitch," Ward snapped, leaving Ben at the doorway. "You could've stopped all this if you'd listened to me."

"Now is not the time for finger pointing, Inspector. Get on that phone and call Reykjavík. We need extra men and paramedics down here, now!"

Anger surged through Ward, to the extent he could feel his eyes almost bulging from their sockets as his hate towards the commissioner burned. "You don't outrank me anymore, you bastard."

"What did you say to me? I'll have your bad—"

"Fuck the badge!" Ward shouted, ripping it from his shirt and throwing it across the room so it landed at Kári's feet. In an instant, he'd cut the distance between them and pressed his forehead against the commissioner's. "You hear me, you prick? Fuck your badge. You sentenced all those people to die by not listening to me. Ingvar, too!"

Kári was about to reply, but Ward got to him first with a solid right to the jaw that sent him to the floor. He was about to warn the man to stay out of his way but the words never left his mouth, as he himself caught a punch to the jaw that saw him knocked onto his back.

What the...? How can anyone move that fast? Fuck this!

He scrambled up and dove on Kári, with both men rolling on the floor, wrestling as they endeavoured to out-muscle each other. At first, Kári dominated, pinning Ward down with his forearm across his neck, but Ward managed to twist out and flip the commissioner onto his back. The pair traded punches – some blocked, others landing without any real power – before they both got back to their feet, each struggling for breath.

Kári glared at him but didn't move. Ward lunged, throwing a flurry of wild swings that didn't really connect, but had him gasping for breath again. Then Kári hit him – the thump, like a loud crack, filling Ward's head – and the strength sank out of his knees as he buckled to the floor, his head thumping off the boards.

Everything went dark, maybe for a few seconds, or hours – he didn't know. When his senses returned, the smell of pine filled his nostrils. His vision was as clear as day and he felt sure his hearing was sharper than before as he focused on the strain his lungs were under as they fought for breath.

"Strike the commissioner?" Kári barked. "You stupid fool." He drew his gun, chambered a round, and pointed it at Ward's head, then leaned down and un-holstered Ward's pistol, which he threw to the floor. "After everything that has happened here tonight, no one would miss you if I dumped your body into that cave."

Ward coughed up a lump and spat it out in a wad of blood. He tongued his cheek and around his mouth, fairly certain a tooth was missing, coughed and spat again, then looked hard at the commissioner. "Go on then, fucking do it."

Kári gave no warning, his boot catching Ward in the face, knocking him back. He roared, his eyes welling up, the bridge of his nose crooked beneath his fingertips. *Fuck this!* He scrambled around, searching for his gun, or baton, or anything that could aid the situation. As he did so, he caught the look on Kári's face. *The bastard's enjoying this.*

The commissioner raised his gun again, the barrel steady as a rock. "Any last words?"

"Go fuck yourself."

Ward closed his eyes and waited for the sound – the same one he'd heard a second before his daughter died. Someone grunted, then the floor shook as something heavy landed on it. He kept his eyes closed.

Am I dead?

Can I now finally be reunited with my beautiful Niamh?

As these thoughts ran through his mind, he realised he was very much alive. He blinked away the tears and saw Kári lying prone and unconscious in front of him.

He scanned the room. Ben sat slumped in the doorway, but a giant of man stood a few feet away, holding Ward's baton. "Rúnar? You crazy son of a bitch."

"I'm just in time," he said, Rakel entering the cabin behind him.

She ran to Ward, assessing his injuries. "You're hurt."

"I've been worse."

"Let me help you."

"I'm fine," he snapped. "Go help him." He nodded at Ben.

"We've got a problem, Inspector," Rúnar said.

Ward watched Rakel aid Ben. Despite his pain, there was something in the way she moved that almost had him fantasising about her again, but he shook his head and focused on what Rúnar was saying. The man was hyper, speaking fast, mixing English and Icelandic as he explained that he witnessed the slime dragging women into the cave. He speculated that, like Ally, those girls were not dead – most likely possessed, or being harvested. Hundreds of them.

"So, what are you saying?"

"I'm saying we need to do something while this thing is still gathering up women." He looked to Ben.

"It's like what I told you about that wasp. It finds a host, using it to reproduce. If we don't stop it now, this village and island are doomed."

FOURTEEN

It didn't take long to get Ben back to his feet. Words of encouragement, a drop of whiskey, and few back pats from the group did the trick. The four of them stood looking down on Kári's unconscious body, passing the bottle in silence, each sipping as they deliberated on what to do with him.

"Fuck it," Ben said, "we should dump the prick outside."

As much as Ward wanted to agree, he restrained himself, knowing that he'd rather keep his enemy in sight. After a few more sips and discussion, they decided it would be best to handcuff him to the radiator, at least for the time being. They each grabbed a limb and shuffled him towards the wall, then Ward cuffed his wrist to the piping coming from the floor.

"Now what?" Rakel asked.

"We find Ally," Ben answered, giving a matter-of-fact shrug.

"She just took off, kid," Ward said. "She could be anywhere."

"She's in that cave with that thing." Ben looked at each of them, his bottom lip trembling. "I know she is. Part of that thing is inside her. Controlling her." He nodded at Rúnar. "You saw the people on the beach, it took those it wanted, and killed—"

"Enough!" Ward snapped, his thoughts shifting to Ingvar, the weight of his sadness lifted by a desire for revenge. It's what the young lad deserved. At least, that's what he kept telling himself. "We can't walk blindly into that cave."

"What are you suggesting?" Rakel's voice quivered, as if she already knew the answer.

"Isn't it obvious?" Rúnar said, looking down at her. "We need to cut the head off the snake."

"Snake?" Ben stared at him. "Ah, if you mean go back down into that pit and get my Ally back, then I'm in." He slapped his fist into his open palm, his eyes wide. "One-hundred percent, mate."

Ward shook his head, about to take another mouthful of whiskey, when he noticed the group looking at him. He lowered the bottle. "What? What the fuck you want from me?"

"Your help would be nice," Rakel snapped. "We'll need the Toyota, and maybe some weapons."

"Take whatever you want. My enemy is cuffed to that pipe, and I'm going to get mine when he wakes up." He glared at Kári and, as if the man heard him, he began to move. At first it was a sharp jerk, then his knees pulled in close to his chest. With a moan, he kicked out, clattering the radiator with a violent thump.

"The prick is awake," Ward said, touching his swollen nose. He went over to examine him, rolled him onto his back, and waited, ready to give him what he deserved. Kári stirred, but didn't fully awaken, his eyes glazed over from the blow to the back of the head. That's when Ward noticed something running down his neck, down beneath his shirt. Black marks, like a sprinkle of pepper. A tattoo? He tore open the shirt to reveal the image. A tattoo, but not the typical tribal type shops advertise in their windows. No, this was highly detailed, almost like branding or scarring on the left side of his chest. Symbols, like swirling scripture in a language he couldn't understand. At its centre was a mismatch of what he could only describe as a black waterfall pouring onto a fallen cross.

"That is very strange," Rúnar said, looking over Ward's shoulder.

"Is it Icelandic?"

"No."

"Nordic?"

"No. I've never seen symbols like this before."

Kári began whispering – low, inaudible – almost whimpering.

"What's he saying?" Ward slapped his face to get him to come to. Without warning, Kári's eyes shot open – jet black, bulging, followed by a hissing from deep within. Everyone recoiled. In one blink, his eyes returned to normal.

Ben gasped. "What the fuck, mate? He's infected with that slime shit."

Ward heard a loud snapping sound – the chain linking the cuffs was broken and the commissioner was free. Rúnar dived in to restrain him but squealed and doubled over, both hands holding his gut. He stood up and backed away, a small knife protruding from his abdomen, his eyes wide in shock.

Kári jumped up and ran for the door, shoving Ben and Rakel out of the way as if they were nothing.

Ward got there just before him and blocked the exit, then acted on impulse, putting all his weight behind a right swing, his knuckles cracking on impact. Such a punch would normally knock anyone down, or even out, but it was like Kári's jaw was made of iron, and his hand felt it, the pain shooting back to his shoulder.

Before he could fully register what happened, something thundered into his chest and the wooden door shattered behind him as he was sent through, landing on his back outside, surrounded by a sea of splinters. His body ached all over, as if he'd just been gored by a rhino. Kári stood a few feet away, his face etched with a murderous glare and grimace. Ward groaned and rolled onto his side, trying his hardest to get to his feet, but before he could, he was lifted from the decking as the rhino rammed him for a second time, and he landed with a thump on the cold tarmac road, gasping for breath.

He struggled to his feet, unsteady but up. Kári ripped his shirt off as he approached, revealing the strange symbols dotted all over his torso. Then, in a blur, his arm shot out and Ward gagged at the power of the man's grip on his throat.

"This is the part where you die," he whispered, squeezing with the force of a vice.

Ward struggled as Kári's hold tightened, his vision sparking as darkness encroached.

This is it. Finally... this is the end.

He was certain he heard bones cracking. Somewhere through his death struggle, noise seemed to erupt from down on the beach. Or was it the sound of his brain losing oxygen? A screeching, similar to the one he'd heard before the slime ran riot outside the cave. It grew louder and he realised he wasn't dreaming or hallucinating. Then he was lifted and his body hit the road again, like a ragdoll. He blinked away his blurred vision, saw a flicker in Kári's eyes – black, almost like a second set of eyelids. The man glared at him, turned to the ocean, looked at him again and, almost serpent-like, leaned back before taking off in the direction of the cave.

FIFTEEN

Ben arrived at the police hut with a bulging rucksack on his back and a petrol canister under each arm. He laid them down beside the radiator.

"Good," Ward said, looking them over while rubbing his neck.

"You think this is going to work?" Ben asked.

"Look at where we are, kid? Does it look like this village is equipped to deal with any sort of conflict? They don't even have a standing army here."

"Alright, mate, I only asked."

"So, we need to make use of what we have. Rakel will be here in a minute and we can get to work."

As if on cue, the police Toyota screeched to halt outside – a loud clinking from the back evoking a knowing look from Ben. Ward didn't hesitate putting the group to work. Rúnar struggled to unload empty beer bottles from the vehicle, while Ward and Ben cleared the floor space in the office.

Rakel insisted that the big man rest, reminding him that the stab wound may have been a minor one but still needed to be looked after. "I didn't patch you up so you could tear your stitches a few hours later."

Rúnar didn't reply. Instead, he sat out of the way and watched them, his look showing that deep down he knew she was right.

Rakel ran a sweeping brush over the floor, and one by one they lined out the bottles. Using a funnel Ward kept to top his Toyota's oil up with, they emptied the canisters into the bottles, then dipped old rags in alcohol and oil, creating a wick for each bottle.

"Voilà, petrol bombs!" Ward announced proudly.

"Don't you mean, Molotov cocktails?" Rúnar corrected.

"Where I'm from, these are known as petrol bombs."

"Aye, he's dead on, mate," Ben said. "But we'll need a bit more bang for our buck. And I know just the thing."

"What are you talking about," Ward asked.

"Give me a few minutes and I'll show you."

As he took the rucksack and went about his work in the bathroom, the rest checked their safety gear: helmets, torches, ropes, and packed it all into the Toyota. When they returned, Ben was on his knees with pliers and a hacksaw, using gunpowder from the shotgun shells and piping from beneath the bathroom sink to construct several pipe bombs.

Ward stood over him and shook his head in admiration. "Fair play – I'd never have thought of that."

"As it stands, these bad boys shred flesh and bone, but we need something extra to give us more clout."

Ward couldn't hide his smile. *Lovestruck tourist, my arse. This kid knows a thing or two.* "What you need, lad?"

He got to his feet. "Well, mate, if you're going to go camping in Iceland, you better pack the right gear. And I know just the thing."

"Take the car. Don't take longer than one hour. You hear me?"

"Aye."

The group continued prepping, crating up the petrol bombs and giving the floor a wipe down. To everyone's surprise, the Toyota pulled up outside roughly twenty minutes after he'd left and the horn sounded. "Give me a hand, mate."

The three of them went out.

"What the fuck?" Ward exclaimed on seeing the back seat loaded with propane tanks. A couple of reams of cotton string, bottles of weed killer, and what looked to be airbags pulled from a car.

"Aye, there's a wee shop over the road. Fully stocked with camping gear. I figured we could do with these more than the lads on the beach, eh?"

Ward scanned the material. "And the airbags? And what's that, weed killer?"

"All airbags need a blasting cap to set them off on impact... The perfect detonator, mate." He said with a cheeky wink, "And a cotton string soaked in weed killer makes the perfect fuse."

Ward didn't reply, but gave him a disapproving look.

"What?" Ben asked, "I'm into fireworks..."

The tanks were hauled inside and Ben went about his work, creating a mix of propane pipe bombs. Then, like a doting father, he stood back and admired his work. "These little Frankies contain enough whack to strike fear into Gerry Adams himself. Am I right, mate?" He looked to Ward.

"Nice work, lad. Seriously, good job. But, what's a Frankie?"

"Frankenstein, mate. I mean, it's not your typical IED, but these lads will blow the fuck out of anything. I'm sure of it."

"What do you do back in the real world?" Rakel asked, her eyes wide with amazement.

"Are you hinting at marching bands and all that jazz, love?"

The room filled with an awkward silence.

Ben chuckled. "Ach, I'm only a drummer, but I was in the Royal Irish Regiment a few years ago. Not for long but I learnt a few tricks from the boys."

The pipe bombs were added to the stash of Frankies and placed into the back of the 4x4. Ward then checked the armoury – if it could even be classed as such. It was more like an oversized foot locker, for all of the available weapons. Slim pickings, but enough to maintain order in Vík in the event of civil unrest – a comical thought that had him rolling his eyes as he laid the arms out on the floor. Two Mossberg 500 pump-action shotguns and two Glock 21 handguns.

"Is that it?" Ben asked.

"This isn't a US platoon, lad. It's all we've got."

He handed a shotgun to Rúnar, with a nod that said, *you look like you know how to use one of these.* Whether that was true or not, Ward didn't want to know. He issued a Glock to Rakel and Ben, then loaded his shotgun and made his way out to the Toyota.

"What's the plan, mate?" Ben asked.

"Go in all guns blazing."

"What about the cold?" Rakel asked.

"Come again?"

"We carried out tests on the organism. It didn't like the cold and reacted violently to extreme heat. If we go in there setting off bombs, don't you think we run the risk of making this situation worse than it already is?"

Ward nodded once. "Ok, I know anti-freeze repelled it, but that won't do. We need to get in deep and blow the thing to kingdom come."

Rakel shook her head, obviously not convinced.

Ward looked down to the beach, towards the mouth of the cave. Snow-heavy clouds loomed and a thick mist was coming in from the sea, but it wouldn't bother them where they were headed. "We're going in. No matter what it costs, we have to stop that fucking slime."

"I don't want to be a martyr," Rakel muttered.

"I'm not forcing anyone to come... but this needs to be done."

She closed her eyes for a moment before looking at him and nodding.

"What about my Ally?"

146

Ward didn't answer. How could he? *Fuck!* If she was possessed by some entity from beyond the stars, how could anyone know what would happen? If they killed the creature, would she die or return to life, as if released from some kind of mind-control? He had to try, no matter what. If not for Alison, then for himself. He'd watched his daughter taken before his eyes. And knowing that pain all too well, there was no way on Earth he was going to let something like that happen again. "Get some rest, folks. We leave at first light."

Flurries of snow blanketed the road and combined with mist, visibility was reduced to no more than a few metres in front of them. This didn't stop Ward flooring the accelerator to reach the cave quicker. The sludge didn't like anti-freeze, he knew that much. But without resources, Ben's Frankensteins would have to suffice. Their meagre plan was backed by sheer determination – tinged by desperation – to enter the cave, seek out the cosmic slime, and do what they could to destroy it.

If we can hurt it, we can kill it.

The sky, a dark grey, seemed to have fallen to the ground, engulfing the 4x4. But, despite the blanketing snow, the air didn't seem as cold as expected, and through the partially open window, birds could be heard, possibly puffins or seagulls, squawking and screaming nearby – the sounds rushing past the jeep, as if they knew what was coming and were fleeing in panic.

As he powered down the road, the wipers struggled to clear the snow from the windscreen. In a split-second of clarity, he caught a glimpse of a woman, clothes soaking wet, her face drooped and partially covered by long black hair. The sickening thud had him slamming on the brakes, the 4x4 swerving and skidding along the snow-slick tarmac, eventually stopping inches from a ditch. Snow danced across the headlight beams as they faced towards nothing but gloomy cloud.

"What the fuck?" Ben cried.

Ward didn't answer. He didn't need to, having seen what happened just like the rest of them. *The poor woman.* His heaving breaths filled the silence

"Everyone stays here," he said, easing the door open, taking his shotgun with him. The snow crunched beneath his boots. He looked back along the fresh skid marks, tiny crystals of light glistening all around him. About ten feet ahead, the body lay, dressed in white.

"Fuck."

He made his way over, but as he got closer, he saw that she was wearing nothing more than a light dress – unheard of in this climate and at this time of year. What was she doing out here alone? Within touching distance, he realised she was still breathing, her arms making small movements. His instinct urged him to assist, but something in the way she moved made him wary. It wasn't a struggle, nor did she seem to be in pain. Instead, she got to her feet and turned to face him – forcing a gasp from him. Her face was paler than snow, eyes bulging, with black goo dripping from them. *What the fuck!* He stood watching as she jerked and lurched towards him, her mouth gaping, with more black liquid dripping out onto her white dress. Her arms, exposed to the elements, were as white as her face, with long black fingernails poised and ready to strike.

"What the fuck are you?"

Her response was to swipe her claw-like nails at him. His instincts kicked in, dodging her hand, then, using the butt end of his Mossberg, he sent her flying back to the ground. She hissed a loud squeal before the horn from the car grabbed his attention. He looked back to see Rakel and Rúnar in a panic, calling to him, but he couldn't make out what they were saying.

The woman grabbed his ankle, squealing, pulling herself closer. Through her garbled groans, the cries from the Toyota became clear: "Run!"

With his senses sharp, he now saw why they were all in a panic – up ahead, more people, like the woman clawing at his leg, emerged from the snow-heavy mist. He lost count as they ran towards him, eyes and mouths dripping with black goo.

"Hurry, John!" Rakel pleaded.

He shook his foot, but the woman held on. Then he stamped hard on her arm with his free foot, heard the bone snap, but no corresponding cry of pain. At least he was free. *Fuck this.* He ran towards the vehicle, but the faster he ran, the quicker it seemed the people were gaining on him. His footing was far from secure on the road, and before he knew what was happening, his face tasted the tarmac.

Fuck! Get up, John. Come on, man. She fucking needs you.

Panting hard, he struggled to his feet, the raving and ranting crowd nearly on top of him.

"Move your ass, John. Come on!" Rakel screamed again.

Adrenaline raced through him, forcing him along the road and into the Toyota, the door slamming behind him. Before he could register what was happening, the horde had surrounded them, hands with black nails scraping against the glass, some screeching a high-pitched wail as they pulled at the door handles, while others vomited black liquid all over the vehicle.

"Get us out of here!" Rakel yelled, prompting Ward into action. The engine fired up with a roar, and he slammed the accelerator to the floor, powering the 4x4 forward. It struggled to force its way through the mass of evil, eventually making it with sickening thuds and thumps as bodies were knocked aside and under. With the path clear, he didn't look back.

"What the fuck?" Ben shouted.

"Tourists," Rúnar said, so calm, Ward suspected the big man was on something.

"Come again?"

"From the festival. The ones it did not kill or drag below. You saw their eyes, right? That substance is in them and using them as a device to spread its seed."

They sat in silence as Ward followed the snow-covered road down to the beach. He laughed to himself at the fact that walking there from the police cabin only took a few minutes, while driving took over ten because the road looped around the large plateau that sat over the cave network.

As they pulled into the car park, an eerie chill greeted them. Something about the way the waves landed under the flurries filled him with despair.

"The screamers won't be far behind us," Rúnar said.

"Which is why we'd better get moving," Ward replied, exiting the vehicle with a grim determination. The road behind was masked with a curtain of cloud, but it didn't prevent them from hearing the screeching and bellowing. "They're coming. Get the gear."

Using bedsheets Ward had sourced, the four of them grabbed everything, wrapping them in poncho-style slings, and hurrying across the beach, through the haze, until they came to the mouth of the cave.

"Rúnar, Ben, take the Frankies and climb up to the top of the cave."

Ben gasped. "What? Why?"

"Because I fucking said so," Ward snapped. "We need to blow the entrance and keep them screaming bastards out of here."

Both men complied. Ward and Rakel shouted encouragement from the middle of the entrance, pointing to what they believed to be the weak points. Ben suggested that two Frankies should be enough to do the job. The bombs were heavy, but he moved with a steely determination, with Rúnar assisting despite his aching midsection. On any other day, the plan would be pure madness, being that it was a protected heritage site. But if they didn't try to stop the slime, then the screamers might claim a lot more victims. And that deep-rooted fear drove each of them forward.

The screamers were now sprinting across the beach towards them. Ward opened fire, pumping round after round into the rushing horde. He backed into the cavern. "Light 'em up!"

Ben clung from the ceiling like a spider monkey, struggling to ignite the raggy fuses. Below, Rakel lit two petrol bombs, ran towards the screamers, and flung them against each side of the cave entrance. The blinding fireball was enough to deter the first line. She raced back, allowing Ward space to pick some of them off with a couple of rounds. As the bodies hit the snow-covered sand, above them, a loud and blinding flash lit up the cave – then a second, thundering like an earthquake. Rock and ice rained down, forcing the group deeper into the shadows. For now, they were safe. But within the narrowing darkness, a primordial evil waited, and Ward had no doubt it would do everything within its power to repel the threat of annihilation.

SIXTEEN

Fear hung around them as they made their way over the hard, cold ground, moving deeper and deeper into the cave network, how far was anyone's guess. The cries from the screamers had long been left behind by the barricade and the layers of rock above the tunnels.

"I'm starting to think this was a bad idea," Rúnar said, hunching over again to avoid clattering his head off the low ceiling.

Ward was tempted to agree, but now that he had a mission, he wasn't going to give up. A young woman needed to be found and brought to safety, and he'd never let what happened to his beloved Niamh happen again.

"It's so c-cold," Rakel said, her teeth chattering.

Ward could tell that spirits were diminishing, with everyone probably fearful of becoming trapped so far beneath ground, then starving to death in an icy tomb – the weight of petrol bombs and the explosive devices in the sling didn't help matters, either. He stopped and leaned against the wall, resting his face in the crook of his arm. As he caught his breath, he thought about everything up to this point. With all his suffering, both physical and mental, he probably should have reviewed his condition when he had the chance, instead of allowing himself to become overwhelmed by revenge and the need to save the girl, then leading three people into potential oblivion. Ben would have come, anyway – he was certain of that. Still, he should've given it more consideration.

His breath fogged the yellow-grey wall. At least the slime here wasn't black. Someone's torch flickered behind him, and Rakel sniffed. Rúnar, too. And that's when he caught it – the smell. Fire? Burning? But not sulphur, as would be expected. Whatever it was, it had no business this far below the surface.

"Where is that coming from?" Ben asked.

"It has to be up ahead," Rúnar answered.

"Don't run," Rakel said, grabbing Rúnar before he made a dash past Ward.

"Why?"

"Could be the sludge. We've seen what it is capable of. Luring us towards it with strange smells isn't exactly out of the realm of probability, now, is it?"

"She's right," Ward said, "let's keep moving, but stay quiet."

"And you're injured," she added, rubbing Rúnar's forearm. "Don't forget that."

"I'll be alright."

Hunched in the low, frigid tunnel, the group worked their way along, moving deeper and deeper, laboured breathing accompanying each physical effort to squeeze themselves and their weapons between rock and ice in the never-ending maze – a mountain of stone above them, the unknown below.

"Any idea how deep we are?" Ben asked

"Deep," Ward answered, unable to provide anything but a vague response. They kept going for what seemed like hours, stopping now and again to rest and take on water. Even if they wanted to turn around, they wouldn't have the physical ability to make it back. The smell of burning had lingered all the way, but now it got stronger.

"Be alert," Ward whispered as he led them around another twist in the tunnel. Ben, Rakel, and Rúnar lumbered behind with the gear.

Ward stopped dead when he rounded another dull slab of rock. A large clearing lay ahead. It was vast, across and up – probably large enough to fit a four-story building. They came out high, looking down into what he hoped to be a dormant caldera. Evidence of lava flow scarred the walls downward to the ground. His nostrils stung with the smell of sulphur and burning, and something else he couldn't get a handle on. Had they travelled so far beneath the surface that they'd ended up...?

He looked behind. "Rúnar, are we under the volcano?"

The big man surveyed the cavern. "Um... it is unlikely, but not impossible, considering the distance we have travelled."

They huddled against a rock on the edge of the sheer drop, sipping water and resting, taking in the awe-inspiring natural wonder around them.

"Guys," Ben whispered, beckoning them to look over the edge, "I think I know where the slime came from."

From their perch, about forty feet above the ground, something unnatural caught Ward's eye. Among the ice and rock, a large black object sat.

Oval-shaped, it's exterior shone as if it were recently polished.

"My goodness," Rakel said, leaning out. "That's certainly not a natural rock formation."

Rúnar shrugged. "Perhaps a capsule or pod that brought the slime here?"

His statement was met with silence.

"It is a plausible hypothesis," he continued, "but we need a closer look to confirm."

As Ben and Rakel figured out a way to descend to the bottom, Rúnar's focus was fixed on the ceiling. He ushered Ward over. "If I'm right and that thing below is indeed from somewhere else, then the roof would suggest that I am correct."

Ward looked down at the black object, then up at the ceiling. "What do you mean?"

"Look at it?" He pointed up. "Does that rock formation look natural to you?"

All Ward could see was rock and ice, with a number of stalactites pointing down at them. "I don't get what you're seeing."

"Something punched its way through that upper level, and those above it, before plunging to the floor below. The ice cover obviously froze over and is now equivalent to permafrost."

"Okay, maybe you're right. But what does it matter?"

"It means that black capsule has crashed landed here... or was brought and placed here... either way, I think we are dealing with something not of this world."

Loose rock and chippings underfoot meant they all held hands as they tackled the steep decent to the caldera. Rúnar led the way, his eagerness to explore the capsule dragging them along at an uncomfortable pace. Next in line was Ben, who linked Rakel, who held onto Ward. Now and again, she looked back at him to smile. Despite everything, she held onto the hope that they'd make it through this and find time to learn more about each other. She hadn't felt this way about anyone in some time.

Ward's reaction confused and disturbed her when he reciprocated with a flirty wink. It wasn't what she'd expected in a desperate situation like this. Yes, she wanted his personal support, maybe with a hint of what might be, but a wink? It baffled her. However, now wasn't the time to dwell on it.

The base of the caldera was lined with red-coloured stone, almost pavement-like. Rúnar remarked straight away that it wasn't a natural type of rock for the depth they were at. It forged a path from where their tunnel ended to another that led off into darkness.

The large black oval looked to be intact. Immaculate, in fact – its glossy surface pristine, without any evidence of impact damage from bursting through the upper levels, leaving Rúnar's theory in doubt. Rakel surveyed its shape and condition. *Was it built here? Or was it made of something unknown to humanity?*

She looked at Rúnar. The big man couldn't hold his excitement, straining to study it. He ran his hand along the surface, as did she. It was smooth, almost gel-like. A texture that reminded her of candle wax.

"This thing is the size of my house," Ben said.

Rúnar nodded. "Maybe it is someone's house." He scrutinized its height and breadth. "If the slime travelled in this... vessel, I would love to know how. Or how it gets in and out of it."

At that point, they realized that it had no sign of entry – no door, keypad, or anything human engineers on Earth would put in place.

Rakel wandered around to the other side of it. "Look! Over here." Dotted along its centre were strange brail-like symbols, almost Nordic looking, but etched into it with a precision she had never seen before.

"Shit, mate. What's all that mean?"

As Rúnar, Rakel, and Ben studied the markings, Ward followed the reddish path, his curiosity getting the better of him. He entered the tunnel, catching a strange smell hanging in the air. Only rock lined the way, the absence of ice setting him to wonder what was so different about this tunnel. He continued on, leaving a trail of mental breadcrumbs at sharp turns and forked passages. Then, without warning, he found himself in another clearing – a vast hollow. Unlike the one previous, this had a noticeable absence of ice, with dull, grey rock spiralling upward into a solid dome-like ceiling. His skin tingled from the heat, and he stopped dead when the reason for it became clear: *Fire.*

Hundreds of burning touches, like something from a beach in Hawaii, or a pagan sacrifice, lined a path across the clearing.

What the fuck? Where am I?

A million things rushed through his head, none of which made any sense. But one thing he was certain of – they were not the only humans down here. Someone had lit the oil lamps, and not too long ago.

Ward followed the lights, a strange mix of burning embers encouraging him forward. He wanted to go back to the others, but needed to explore more. *If someone put these lamps in here, they must have come in some other way. Another entrance... but also, an exit.*

The air became dank – foul – like rotten eggs, and something else he was sure he'd smelt before but couldn't remember. He made a point of being quiet as the path led into another tunnel. Strange markings ran along the walls, not unlike the ones on the black object. He'd seen them somewhere else, too, but for the life of him he couldn't pin it down.

The air in here is melting my brain.

Then a sound reverberated through the tunnel, and he stopped, his torch lighting the ground around him as he listened. *What the fuck is it?* He moved forward and, as he progressed, it became clearer – a mix of moaning, crying, and drone-like chanting. The tunnel curved to the right, and he switched off his torch as light spread across the floor and walls. He kept his back to the wall, his shotgun at the ready as he side-stepped towards the opening. *Fuck it, I should've gone back.* But it was too late now. When he followed the bend, another clearing greeted him, circular in shape, just like the last one, only this time the dome was alive with a hive of activity.

He crouched behind a large rock, peeking out to see what was going on. People, loads of people. All women. Tourists from the festival but not like the infected ones they'd encountered back on the road.

No, these were still very much human, but pinned against the cavern's walls by the sludge. Their whimpering created a warped harmony beneath the droning as they struggled to break free from the slime's grip. But it was useless – they were going nowhere. Squelching noises followed every cry, as if the slime was re-enforcing its hold on them.

Ward studied every aspect of the situation, analysing each sound and movement. But something was missing – the drone-like chanting, and he couldn't figure out where it was coming from. He spotted another tunnel entrance on the far side of the cavern. That had to be the source of it. Moments later, his suspicion was confirmed when figures emerged from its opening, clad in black robes, chanting something low and indecipherable. All faces were covered by hoods, with each person holding a burning stick.

The droning grew louder as they formed a large circle in the centre of the clearing, their torches held high. The collective glow filled the cavern, with all surfaces radiating as if red hot, burning into the futile struggles of those trapped along the wall.

Another person emerged from the tunnel and walked into the centre of the circle. The chants grew louder as the hooded figure raised both arms, and that's when it dawned on Ward that he was witnessing some sort of ritual.

The central figure, a man by his voice, was chanting something different to the rest of the group, beckoning to the walls and the tunnel entrance. Then the chanting stopped and he began hissing.

Ward's ears hurt when a screeching noise filled the space, coming from the tunnel. Then goosebumps erupted all over him as a steady flow of black oil squelched and bubbled from the entrance and flowed into the clearing, parts of it linking with the sludge along the walls, the rest pulsating and rising before the person in the middle.

He removed the hood, his back to Ward. Definitely a man. He announced something in Icelandic and the slime appeared to stop and obey him.

Ward was sure he knew him, but he had to be certain. He pulled his shotgun close and shifted along the ledge to get a better look, but he didn't need a full view to know.

"Kári..."

You son of a bitch. What the...? What is this shit?

Too many questions raced through his head as he struggled to comprehend what he was looking at. He wanted to take aim and send a piece of hot lead through his head, but resisted the urge.

Kári began chanting again, the slime seemingly reacting to every word, as if he were a snake charmer. Then the ritual began. More hooded people emerged from the tunnel, dragging a man with them. The distraught guy screamed, obviously pleading for his life in whatever language he spoke. As if in direct reaction, the slime around the walls activated, almost boiling, its captives moaning and groaning in terror. The prisoner was forced before Kári, whose chanting became more aggressive.

Ward recognised him. The chef from the grill. Kári touched him on the forehead, leaving a black mark. The slime froze for a second, as if thinking, like a cobra about to strike, then launched itself onto the man. His screams only lasted a couple of seconds as the black death forced its way down his throat. A moment later, his eyes bubbled black, and his nails stretched like black talons. Then a low hum reverberated off the walls as he was clad in a black robe by the others and placed among the ranks.

Two more men were brought centre stage. Ward didn't get what he expected. Gaps appeared within the goo's 'head' and teeth-like shards formed. Without ceremony, it split and lunged at the men, tearing them apart in seconds, leaving a pool of human entrails on the ground.

Shocked, but holding himself together, Ward couldn't figure why these were destroyed and others chosen.

It's like some sort of fucked up rite of passage.

The chanting returned. Louder, almost celebratory. He scanned the prisoners along the wall, stopping at a woman. Even though her eyes bulged as she vomited black sludge, there was no mistaking her. *Alison.* He was sure of it. She looked as if she was in a trance, possessed by the slimy entity.

He'd seen enough. Time to get the others. One way or another, Kári and the slime had to be stopped. No matter the cost.

SEVENTEEN

It took him a while to navigate the tunnels by
memory, having to backtrack twice after heeding his
instincts, but he eventually re-joined the rest of his
crew. They stood in disbelief at his revelation, and
he couldn't blame them. As bad as dealing with an
intergalactic slime monster was, now they had to
deal with some sort of ancient underground cult
who worshipped the thing, as well as sacrificing
innocent people to it. All happening on top of a
volcanic caldera or sealed vent that led down into
the boiling belly of the Earth. This was the reality of

their situation. Coming to terms with it was one thing, now they had to hatch a plan to stop it. And what if they didn't? What could Kári do with that thing on the surface? A scary thought.

"The caldera," Rúnar said.

"What about it?"

"That is how we can end this nightmare. This tunnel network is made up of old fissures and vents that lava would have burst through in previous eruptions."

"The heat is probably why the slime likes it down here?" Rakel said.

"And the cold is why it can only surface sporadically from the cave," Ward added. "Thank fuck for Icelandic weather, eh?"

"Right," Rúnar continued, "it loves the heat, but extreme heat is another thing altogether and nothing can survive lava from a magma chamber. If we can blow the caldera open, we might trigger a lava surge that will flood the interior. It would incinerate everything."

"Probably us, too," Ben said.

Nobody answered, which signalled collective agreement. Rúnar's plan made sense in theory. If the caldera was indeed sitting on top of a vent, then blowing the cap, exposing the magma chamber, was as good a plan as any – like a giant pimple being popped.

"How many Frankies we got?" Ward asked.

"Four, mate."

It wasn't an ideal number but, with the pipe and petrol bombs, they'd have to make do. They crept through the tunnel system, Ward leading, confident that he knew the way now. As they drew closer, the chanting grew louder, then someone screamed.

Silence followed.

Ward looked back at his crew, each horrified by what they'd heard. He shook his head. *That bastard's going to kill them all. The lunatic needs to be stopped.*

When they reached his observation rock, the people in robes were gone. Ben wanted to run to Alison's aid but Ward held him back, telling him they needed to follow their plan. In the centre of the clearing, the caldera was covered in a red dust. The heat, almost akin to a sauna, had sweat running down their faces.

"We'll need to split up," he whispered. "Ben and I will sneak around the base. We'll plant a Frankie as close as we can. That'll be enough to distract them and hopefully cause a panic."

"Good. What about us?" Rakel asked, nudging Rúnar.

"See up there?" Ward pointed to the ceiling, about forty feet up, "You need to go back into the tunnels and make your way up there. Use the remaining bombs to blow that fucking roof. Run the fuse-spool back down here to give yourself enough time to get back to us. The falling rock and explosions below will hopefully be enough to pierce the floor, and then—"

"Then what, mate?"

"Then we all enter the ninth circle of Hell."

As with Ben's comment earlier, nobody said a word. The harsh reality was more than enough. They all looked at each other and nodded. This was a suicide mission. The plan – if it worked – would kill everything down here, and no one anywhere else in the world would even know. What choice did they have?

Ward and Ben waited for what felt like an eternity. Ben's focus never left Alison, but Ward watched the ceiling, waiting for Rakel or Rúnar to appear and begin rigging the devices. He knew the northerner was struggling against the urge to run to his partner, and he couldn't blame him, seeing her pinned to the wall by the sludge – the love of his life, head hung low, drooling black fluid.

"We need to hurry, Inspector."

"Patience, kid. I know it's tough but you have to have patience."

Something shuffled above, and he spotted Rakel's head poking out through a gap in the rock near the ceiling. They'd made it and, more importantly, they'd done so undetected. "See, Ben, now we're ready. They've their job to do and we've ours."

The two of them got to work. They circled the edges of the caldera and planted a Frankie in positions they hoped would cause maximum damage.

"I hope your creations will work, lad."

"Listen, mate, two of these bad boys took down the cave entrance with ease. And they were only five-kilo jobs. The others are ten. It's going to rain fire in here, I promise ye."

"Alright, let's do this."

"Aye, dead on."

Ward was wiring a fuse when muttering came from behind him. One of the women pasted to the wall was awake and trying to signal for help, despite the black goo doing its horrible thing inside and over her. He hesitated but her moans rose, and others woke up, their cries and feeble attempts at screaming filling the cavern.

"Fuck, those nutjobs will know something's happening." He signalled to Ben to pull back behind the rock at the tunnel entrance.

As they crouched there, more slime poured into the space from the other tunnel and rose into a cobra-like blob, shifting from left to right, as if sniffing the air. Tentacles shot out and connected with the goo stuck to the wall, pulsating as its serpent-like movements scanned along the line of captives, obviously searching for the origin of the sound. Then, without warning, a young woman was released and dragged before the 'standing' blob. A gaping smile appeared, meeting her face-on. She was in a daze, but screamed in horror when she realized that the monster's head was now filled with a set of dagger-like teeth.

Seconds later, her screams were cut off when the mouth clamped over her face, the only sound echoing in the vast clearing now was that of crunching and squelching as the blob chewed on her, with dark blood squirting in every direction. Her body hit the hot red dust moments later, her limbs twitching as if in protest at the grotesque act perpetrated on her.

Once the commotion died down, the chants returned – low, almost inaudible, but rising fast, signalling to Ward that the hooded group were making their way back to the cavern.

"Shit," he whispered, "keep your head down. We're not blowing anything until Kári is in the middle."

"And when we get Alison away," Ben added, a deep frown shadowing his eyes, possibly showing his annoyance at Ward not mentioning her.

Kári emerged from the entrance, arms raised idol-like. The others followed, marching into the centre and forming a circle. Then a stick was brought out from beneath each robe, set alight, and raised above their heads.

Another ritual?

Ward did a quick count of the prisoners remaining on the wall. Alison and a few others. *We can't blow the Frankies if they're still stuck to that dammed wall.*

Ben must have read his mind because he whispered the same thing in his ear. He signalled for the northerner to stay down. While they had a plan of action, in reality, he didn't have a single notion how they were going to accomplish it.

A makeshift altar, with a flat slab of stone, was constructed in the circle, and the hooded adherents continued chanting, ready for Kári's next instruction. The slime oozed around his feet, like a pet dog waiting for its master's command.

Kári raised his arms and signalled for silence. Then, for the first time, he spoke English to his followers. "The time has come for our order to fulfil our life's work. For years we have nurtured our saviour. Made sacrifices. Helping regain strength. Waiting for this day... Behold the Dark."

His followers cheered.

"At last we are ready. And I have been chosen! Chosen to become *one* with our glorious saviour. And together we will unite and we shall take this corrupted world into a new and magnificent age."

More cheering as his followers removed their shrouds, revealing the faces of police officers and citizens of Vík – Ward recognized most of them instantly. They all rejoiced at Kári's announcement, dropping any form of religious pretence or ritual.

"Today is judgement day. A day of reckoning and cleansing. And we shall annihilate those who do not follow."

He knelt and pulled a crystal goblet from a pocket of his robe. Next, he held it out and moved it from left to right, as if about to perform a magic trick. Then he scooped up a lump of the slime and held it above his head, spoke in Icelandic, projecting his words in an intense and almost operatic manner, as if psyching up for what he was about to do. All around him gave him their full focus. Then, with a sinister look, he screamed, "Let the blackening of this world begin!"

The command was met with a deafening roar of approval from his followers as they watched him gulp down the contents of the goblet.

Chanting began... "Behold the Dark... Behold the Dark... Behold the Dark..."

At first, he seemed fine, wiping the excess sludge from his mouth but, moments later, he jumped to his feet, his body jerking like he'd been electrocuted or struck by a bolt of lightning. He dropped to his knees and rolled into a foetal position, kicking and screaming in what sounded like absolute agony. After about a minute, the screams stopped and an eerie silence filled the cavern. The faces of his followers conveyed a doubtful hope that the worst had happened, but with a snake-like swagger, almost without effort, Kári rose to his feet, standing tall and strong before them. His robe dropped to the ground, revealing his tattooed body, his physique strong and muscular – his shiny black nails long and tapering. His eyes shone black as he scanned his circle of minions, a low drone emanating from deep within him.

One of the worshippers shouted "Rejoice" over and over again. The rest soon joined in, a droning mix of Icelandic and English.

"Hear me now. I am one with our saviour. Using the best of what our two species have to offer, we shall use this day to mark the dawn of a new era. One in which man will become enhanced and united in one common goal."

A chorus of cheers greeted their leader's words, the slime seemingly now answering to every move Kári made.

"We're fucked, mate," Ben whispered.

The words triggered something in Ward. He glanced over to Alison, then whispered to Ben, "You go get her. Head for the main tunnel and get out of here. The others should be ready, and if they've any sense, they won't be far behind you. Once those fuses are rigged and we light one, there is no going back."

"What about you?"

Ward looked down at Kári. "I've a score to settle."

He was about to move off but Kári's voice stopped him in his tracks, ordering the slime to bring one of the girls before him. A discernible pulse ran along the sludge, up to Alison's place on the wall, and she was released – her weakened body placed in front of Kári.

She stirred, as if activated by an unheard voice, positioning herself on the slab in front of Kári, her legs spread – inviting him.

What the fuck?

Ward deliberately didn't look at Ben.

Kári didn't hesitate, signalling to his followers to leave through the tunnel. As soon as he was alone with Alison and the slime, a long black tentacle extended from where his penis should have been, flickering like a serpent about to attack its prey, closing in on Alison's splayed vulva, her body soaking in sweat from the heat.

Ward had seen enough. He grabbed Ben by the arm. "You save your girl as soon as I have Kári clear."

Ben didn't argue. Ward got up and whistled, after which there was no going back. The fate of the world – humanity as they knew it – was at stake.

EIGHTEEN

"Hey, Dickhead!" Ward shouted, stepping out from behind the rock, catching Kári's attention.

"John Ward..." he snarled. "I thought you would have killed yourself by now."

"Move away from the girl," Ward demanded.

"I'm afraid I cannot do that." Each word came out warped – echoing – as if he had two voice boxes working in unison – a frightening effect. "Behold the Dark, Mister Ward. For today is a new day. The dawn of a new era. Let the blackening of this world begin–"

"Shut the fuck up." Ward lifted the spool of fuse wire. "A single match and this place and your doomsday cult get melted out of existence. Now, hand over the girl."

Kári's eyes bulged, his muscles rippling. He stepped back and let out a roar that hurt Ward's ears. Then, his phallic tentacle shot forward like a stretched elastic, and before Ward knew what was happening, it had coiled around his torso, dragging him towards the commissioner.

He struggled against the slimy member but it was no use, it was too powerful. Kári's black nails extended into tentacles that slithered forward and wrapped around Ward's arms and legs.

They pinned him to the warm ground, and the original slime blob rose behind Kári, becoming still, as if awaiting instruction to lunge forward and mutilate him.

While Ward prepared to die, he spotted Ben from the corner of his eye. He'd somehow made it to Alison unseen and was dragging her to the side of the caldera.

Fuck, if I don't stall this nutjob, we'll all perish.

He waited until Kári's face was close to his, then spat, but got no reaction from the hybrid.

"Kári, you're a fool. What makes you think you can control the slime?"

The commissioner contemplated the question for a second, then, as if commanded telepathically, the slime moved forward, forming a pulsating blob in front of Ward. A slit appeared, revealing pointed black teeth, then it lunged and stuck to the side of his head. He howled in agony, and although he couldn't touch it, he knew his ear was gone. Blood poured from the wound, the mutilation met with laughter by Kári.

He leaned close to Ward's good ear. "Can't be controlled? I am one with this beautiful organism. Don't you understand it yet, John? This creature is not from our world. It was a gift – its creator from beyond the stars, thousands of years ago. They came from vast distances to find those worthy of our saviour."

"How do you know it wasn't just abandoned here?" Ward snapped, the gushing blood hot on his neck. "Maybe they couldn't control it and decided to get rid of it?"

"Ha, don't be a fool. Who do you think has been watching over our saviour? We are keepers of the Dark, and we are the shepherds, protecting our beloved dating back to the first people on this island. We have been trusted as its guardians since the formation of parliament in Þingvellir. For generations, we have protected it. Until now. Freed by the heat of Katla, free from imprisonment, nurtured back to strength, the time has come for you and the rest of this inconsiderate race you call humanity to be purified." His black eyes bulged.

A thin tentacle shot out from his ear, crawled up to the bloody hole where Ward's ear used to be, and inserted itself, triggering intense, agonising screaming. Then, as if transported to another dimension, Ward found himself in a dream-like state, watching the world from a bird's-eye view.

Below him was Iceland, he was sure of that, but it looked so different to the modern-day island. It almost had a prehistoric feel to it. *This bastard is implanting memories in my head.* Vikings or Norsemen appeared on what he assumed was a law rock in the misty land. They spoke a language he couldn't understand, but knew from their demeanour that the discussion was over something serious. He studied them, trying to decipher their words through actions, and it dawned on him that Kári was showing him the arrival of the star men. They'd arrived from the sky like a shooting star. The black capsule landed on the path beside a drowning pool. One of the Vikings stepped forward, lowering his axe, and appeared to argue with the strange beings. Then, as if a deal had been brokered, the Viking was pinned to the ground and his clothing torn from his chest. Using a single black nail, the being carved a scripture into his skin. The warrior screamed in pain, and when he stopped, the beings vanished into the misty rain as fast as they'd come, leaving the capsule behind. The Viking wore his new wound like a badge of honour.

The Dark was created that day, and had existed ever since – a secret that only the chosen few knew about. Time advanced, through many volcanic eruptions, and the blackened land evolved to one of natural beauty, where villages and towns were eventually built. The capsule was carried great distances by those in robes – hundreds of them, digging and eventually hiding it beneath Katla. There he saw it shine black within the soaring heat, the slime sweating out of it and then his head filled with the sharpest pain he'd ever experienced and all he could do was scream at the top of his lungs in the hope that he could force it out of his head. When he thought he was about to die, the pain vanished and he returned to himself, breathless and struggling to focus on the half-man, half-monster standing before him.

"Behold... the Dark."

Ward rolled his eyes, using the reaction to take in his surroundings. No sign of Ben or Alison anywhere. He'd earned them a head start and that was good enough for him. "You're a fool, Kári. It'll only consume you like it does everyone else."

His words were met with rage. The slime shot forward again, this time snapping down on Ward's left hand.

"Aaaaaaagggggghhhhhhh!"

Kári laughed like a maniac.

Ward looked around in panic. *My fucking hand!* He was a bloody mess, convinced he'd bleed out in minutes. To his horror, he saw the slime drag Rakel down from the tunnel. She fought, but was unable to gain any ground over the cosmic sludge.

Kári laughed harder now, his black eyes whirling with madness.

She was placed alongside Ward, who pleaded with Kári, but the commissioner didn't flinch. Instead, his face split in half, revealing two slimy stalks, like slug eyes rising up. On the tips, small spores pulsated, and Ward knew he was going to implant them in her. Both prisoners screamed in terror.

"Close your eyes, Rakel," Ward shouted.

A harrowing scream boomed around the caldera. Kári recoiled in agony, clutching what was left of his face, with one of the stalks lying motionless on the ground.

Ward looked about. *What the fuck?*

Then their slimy binds loosened, allowing them both to wriggle free. They pushed themselves away from the monster as it convulsed and thrashed about in front of the tunnel entrance, the slime blob behind, mimicking its every move. And that's when Ward realized what had happened.

Rúnar, the big man, clung to Kári's back, slashing and stabbing him over and over with a jagged knife. Chunks of black slime ejected from every wound, screeching and screaming, with Kári bucking like a rodeo horse in efforts to dislodge him.

Using his remaining hand, Ward grabbed hold of Rakel and they helped each other back behind the safety of the rock.

Aghast at the bloody mess before her, she torn a strip off her shirt and tied the rag around his upper arm.

Kári eventually got Rúnar on the ground.

Rakel wanted to run to him, but Ward held her back. "Don't, Rakel, that thing will kill us all. Rúnar's doing what he needs to do."

They watched in horror as the good stalk spluttered spores all over Rúnar's face, causing him to fall into a gagging and coughing spasm. Kári's laughter, once sounding human, now came as a demonic cackle. As Rúnar struggled to his feet, the slime and Kári begin a merging process – the slime entering his body, morphing him into a large human-slime mutant creature.

Using one of its many tentacles, it grabbed Rúnar by the leg, held him up to inspect him, then flung him across the caldera, his body slamming into the wall like a ragdoll.

The creature screeched, almost in triumph, slithering, bubbling, and pulsating.

"Now what do we do," Rakel whispered. "That thing will tear us to shreds."

Through the throbbing pain, Ward noticed his bleeding had subsided, but he had to cauterize the wound if he was to survive. Priorities first, though. He scanned the caldera. The creature was too big to fit into the tunnel, unless it could change from a blob into slime form? He assumed it could. "We have to try and keep it in here. You have to light the fuse."

NINETEEN

The tunnels twisted and turned for what seemed like an age – the walls cold and icy –progress being all the more difficult with the dead weight of Alison on his shoulder. Ben used the light on his phone to guide the way, hoping and praying that the entrance would reveal itself at the next turn. He'd been climbing for so long now, his energy levels were critically low, like his phone. Despite its diminishing battery, he hoped to get a signal soon to make that call to have Ally air-lifted to a hospital.

Exhaustion dragged behind him like an anchor. Occasionally, he stopped to check Ally, always limp and unconscious, with that horrible black goo dried all over her from where it had leaked. *Is there a way to get the stuff out of her? Or is she doomed to stay in that catatonic state?* Each time, he took a deep breath, hoisted her back onto his shoulder, and worked himself forward, one step at a time, always hoping for the best.

With every twist and turn in the labyrinth, all he came across was more rock, more coldness, and that constant dank stench in the air. Then the notification on his phone beeped, signalling the battery was down to its last bar. *Shit!* Despair gripped him, its hold cold as ice. He'd come this far, saved Alison, and now, as they made their way to the surface, light had become their biggest enemy. Not the alien-human hybrid or the rigged cavern – no, it was the simplest of things that he took for granted. Light. Without it, they'd be left to die in this cold dark tomb.

His light flickered, then a second time, and before he could get his bearings, the phone died.

"No, please, no!" He shifted Alison into his arms and crouched down, his back to the wall, doing his utmost to stop tears of desperation from bursting forth. "It wasn't meant to be this way, baby. I swear. This trip was supposed to be one of the highlights of our lives. I wanted so bad to go home and tell all our family and friends the big news. And to see you in your white dress – my bride, my love, with the biggest smile on your beautiful face. I'm so sorry, Ally."

He held her in a tight but gentle embrace, wishing to see in the pitch darkness, though he knew he was wasting his time. *What's the use? We're fucked.* He ran his fingers over her face, using the lightest touch, mentally mapping it as he tried to get a clear picture of her in his mind. No reaction. *You always loved when I did this to you.* He kissed her forehead, closed his eyes, and stifled a groan as a shiver ran through him.

He nuzzled his head against Alison's and, for a moment, his eyelids became heavy and a flurry of memories raced through his mind, all blasted away by a screeching, growl-like sound that shocked his head back against the wall, but reminded him of the noises he'd heard back on the road when Ward had knocked the girl over.

It came from deep in the darkness, sometimes faint but then it would grow in intensity and volume. Then his breath caught when Alison's lips moved against his fingertips. *Is she trying to talk?* He couldn't see, only feel.

"Ally? Ally? Are you awake?"

She didn't reply, but the low moaning kept coming from his left, up the tunnel. Something was happening and he couldn't see. He got to his feet and hoisted her onto his shoulder, holding her firm with one arm while using the other to navigate the tunnel by feeling the wall.

Slow step by slow step, he worked his way forward. The moans and groans grew louder. Something or someone was up ahead – he could sense it and it scared the shit out of him but his survival instinct willed him on.

"I'm going to get you out of here, Ally. I promise."

He took a deep breath and held it to listen, but his heartbeat in his ears thundered over the sounds ahead. About a minute later, they changed, becoming clearer. He tried to keep his hopes in check, but couldn't help think that it was a busload of tourists all chattering together, trying to get snaps of whatever natural attraction was above the tunnel network.

Without warning, his guiding hand fell forward, with nothing to press against. He stopped, afraid he'd come to the edge of a massive drop, though he couldn't remember passing one on the way in. With no other choice, he inched one foot forward in the hope of touching solid ground. Relieved to find there was, he took a couple of short steps forward, then a blind left-to-right wave of his hand found a sharp turn in the system and, with it, a faint light in the distance.

"Oh, my God. Ally, wake up. We're almost there. C'mon, baby, stay with me here!"

Adrenaline kicked in and his fatigue disappeared. The sound, almost buzzing, became clearer with nearly every step, the light growing brighter and brighter until he was able to make out a square white hole at the end of the tunnel. Only a few more feet and they'd be back on the surface.

Moving into the light was like stepping into what he believed heaven would feel like. White light, all around him. Blinding. Initially hindered by the glare, his sight adjusted with the help of a series of rapid blinks.

"We made it, baby."

He placed her on the ground and rubbed his eyes. She stirred, but whatever she mumbled didn't register with him. He wasn't bothered. At this moment in time, all that mattered was they were so close to salvation. His vision was clear and the fresh air gave him a burst of energy. He stood to his full height but balked when he saw what was causing the sound. A busload of tourists? No. The motor in a car engine? No. It was nothing that brought him joy. The entrance and the light lay ahead but, to his horror, he realized that his nightmare was far from over.

Hundreds of people: tourists, police officers, and even figures in black robes, all stood around. Some grumbled and bickered, others remained silent, with the odd outburst of screeching here and there.

He covered his mouth to prevent his panicked gasps being heard. They hadn't seen him, but his hopes were shattered at the sight of the cave entrance blocked off, apart from the light seeping in at the top. All the people, infected by the slime – all with black eyes and long nails – standing around as if waiting for a command, or something to trigger the horde into action.

He retreated back into the tunnel, pulling Alison underarm with him, stopping just out of view.

"Fuck. There's no way out. We're doomed. We're all doomed." They couldn't go forward and there was no way they could move back into the belly of the mountain. He lay her down, took a deep breath, and then the tears came, hard and heavy, and all he could do was rest his face in his hands, battling within himself – coming to terms with a heavy, inevitable decision.

"Ally, babe... I love you. Forever." He tensed his mouth shut to prevent a howl of torment and regret escaping, then removed his jacket and folded it as tight as possible. With one last look, he pressed down hard on her face with it. She struggled beneath his weight, kicking and scraping, but he put all his remaining energy behind it and, soon, whatever strength she had diminished and she became still and limp, leaving him crying alone in the darkness.

TWENTY

The heat from the caldera was becoming unbearable. Ward's lungs burned and sweat stung his eyes. Rakel was struggling with it, too, and he kept urging her to go light the fuse, but she wanted to tend the wounds where his ear and hand used to be. "We can't let that thing leave the cavern," he said.

She looked at him, her eyes red, tears trailing down her cheeks. "I have to fix your... wounds."

"Rakel, my dear, look at me." He held her wrist. "I don't have much time here. Even with the tourniquet, it's likely that I'll bleed out, and there is nothing you can do to stop it. We're miles below the surface. I'm done."

"No, you're not, John. Your legs are fine. Stand up. Come on, stand up. I'm going to get you out of here." She pulled and pushed at him until he was on his feet. He decided not to protest – doing the right thing, however futile, would make her feel better. They looked around the rock and saw that the creature was still fusing – human and slime becoming one. A process that must take time, Ward assumed. Either way, it didn't look as if it was paying much attention to them.

"Do we need to distract it?" Rakel asked, looking around their immediate area.

"Ha, I don't think so. Look..."—he almost laughed— "the big crazy bastard has still got some fight left in him."

Rúnar was struggling to his feet, no longer coughing.

"He's one tough bastard."

"Sure is. Poor Rúnar. What is he doing?"

He stumbled over to the creature and Ward couldn't believe it when the big man started calling the slime out.

"The crazy fool is picking a fight!" Rakel said, hand over mouth.

Ward gripped her arm. "That's our cue. Light the damn fuse and let's get out of here."

The slime creature had formed into a giant half-man, half-blob, resembling a black squid. Rúnar stood before it, roaring abuse.

All the while, Rakel crawled along the cavern's inner wall, the tip of the fuse in sight.

"This place is rigged to go boom!" Rúnar shouted at the creature. He clutched his rib cage, no doubt damaged from the impact against the wall – the stab wound open, oozing black goo. The mutant seemed to understand him, but whatever ability Kári had to speak was lost within the mass of sludge. Tentacles shot forward, grabbing Rúnar and hoisting him up ten to fifteen feet in the air. He winced and fell into a coughing spasm, spewing gloop from his mouth and nostrils. The monster brought him nearer, as if assessing him.

"Time for you to be incinerated, you piece of shit," Rúnar barked, his eyes bulging black, fit to burst.

Ward looked along the wall to see that Rakel had reached the fuse. Considering the length of the spool, he figured she'd only have about four or five minutes before the spark reached the first pipe.

She looked to Rúnar.

Fuck, she wants to save him from that bastard. Not a chance. Those spores are already in him. "What are you waiting for?" he roared. "Light the fucking thing!"

The creature, alerted to their presence, shot tentacles from its side towards Rakel. She screamed as they swiped at her, and Ward urged her on as she fumbled to spark her Zippo into life.

Ward took a deep breath. "Light it and run!"

His breath caught when more tentacles clamped onto the first set. *What the fuck?* He followed them back to their source. They were protruding from Rúnar's fingertips.

"I... can't... hold them... forever," Rúnar shouted, his ribs audibly cracking from the pressure of the creature's grip, his skin bubbling, as if his insides were about to burst through.

Ward thought he saw a small flare of light.

"Got it!" Rakel screamed. The fuse sparkled and fizzled.

"Go! Now!"

She raced back across the caldera towards Ward, while Rúnar roared, obviously using all his strength to hold back the creature in a tangle of tentacles. The entity screeched as it watched them escape into the tunnel. Ward stopped to look back.

The creature bubbled and a head appeared from within, resembling Kári, but mixed with black slime and teeth. It wrapped more tentacles around Rúnar and drew him towards it, its mouth now gaping, its teeth ready.

Using his tentacles, Rúnar shot forward, wrapping them around the creature's teeth, forcing its mouth wider, but also preventing himself from being decapitated. "This... caldera gives the slime energy." He pulled the mouth wider. "I know you know that."

The creature replied with a high-pitched screech.

"The Earth's... energy..." —Rúnar coughed, spewing more black goo—"does not only give you power, but me... too."

More squealing and screeching.

"You fused with Kári, now... fuse with me, you... bastard!"

As soon as the words left his mouth, his face split in half, with two stalks appearing, tipped with spores.

Ward was glad Rakel wasn't there to witness it.

The creature tried to close its mouth, but Rúnar managed to keep it open, then spat the spores into it. The noise was deafening as the creature recoiled, mutating from man to slime, to man again, bucking and trashing all around the caldera.

Rúnar then launched more tentacles, wrapping the creature at every point, fusing himself to it, becoming one giant black blob, eventually easing to a halt in the centre of the caldera – a pulsating mess battling within itself – watching the fuse fizzle forward, waiting for extinction. It looked at Ward.

"Run!"

TWENTY-ONE

Rakel helped Ward along the tunnel, taking the cold, narrow passages that lead in any way upwards. "Hurry, it's going to blow." He kept the bloody stump elevated, across his chest. She had packed it with material torn from their clothing – not ideal, but enough to keep it covered. And with the tourniquet, the danger of bleeding out had been avoided for now, but the threat of infection was real – not that it mattered if they were about to be blown to smithereens.

They hurried along, using the small torch Rakel had brought with her. It gave just enough light for them to navigate the twists and turns.

"What if the creature stopped the fuse?" she kept asking.

"We don't have time to think about that now. We can't go back."

"And Rúnar?"

"He's a brave man."

She kept checking her watch, which he thought useless considering they both knew how fast time was ticking down for the fuse to reach the first Frankie. Still, he had to ask.

"How long have we got?"

"I don't know."

"Fuck."

"Are we far enough away yet?"

"If the explosion works, these tunnels will be flooded in no time."

They continued on, the gradient growing steeper, their energy weaker.

Rakel tugged him. "Look!"

They stopped at a sharp turn and stared into light beyond the tunnel exit.

"Oh, thank God, John, we made it."

However, her excitement didn't last. Ward put his finger to his lips and stepped ahead of her. Two bodies lay on the ground a short distance away.

Rakel gasped. "No, John, is that... Ben and Alison?"

"I think so. Stay here."

"But why did they stop there?"

"Just hold on here." As he made a tentative approach, a whimpering came from the bodies.

"Foster? Is that you lad?" He glanced back at Rakel, then moved forward. "Everything okay?"

Ben didn't reply, just tucked himself closer to Alison, weeping and moaning. Ward shot Rakel a look and mouthed, "What the fuck?"

She made her way over and crouched beside Ben, one hand on his shoulder and two fingers on his wrist. He shivered in response and turned his head to look at her. "There's no escape. We're all going to die. I had to do it, I just had to."

Ward shook his head and walked to the next bend, which he knew led to the cave entrance. *Why did he stop short?* Even with the glare, it didn't take him long to discover the answer. *Oh, fuck! How the hell are we going to get past all of them?*

He crept back to see Rakel trying to comfort Ben, but he wouldn't let go of Alison.

"I had to do it, I just had to. She'd suffered enough."

"Shush, lad. If they hear us, this tunnel with be overrun with those fucking screamers."

Rakel straightened up, her eyes wide as she touched Alison's body. "She's…"

Ward looked at her, then down at Alison. "Shit, what did you do?"

"I had to do it, mate. She couldn't go on like that. I didn't want her to become one of them."

Rakel covered her face with her hands. "He killed her. After all we've gone through to save her."

Ben continued holding Alison, muttering the same words over and over.

Anger boiled in Ward. He'd done everything to save the girl. *What about Ingvar? Rúnar? All for fucking nothing.*

"Right, Foster, I'll deal with you later. For now, we're all going to sneak down that hill and get past those things. And once we're clear, we're going to run like hell."

Rakel checked her watch. "We're running out of time."

They helped Ben to his feet and looked down at all the possessed wandering aimlessly about.

"Without Kári giving the orders, I don't think they're alert to us, or anything else. Let's move down the side and see if we can find a way through the rocks."

"I'm not going anywhere, mate," Ben shouted.

Ward felt the tug at his side, and next he was looking down the barrel of his Glock.

"Lad?"

"Ben? What are you doing?" Rakel asked, holding Ward's good arm.

Ben pointed the handgun at them both and backed down the tunnel. "I told you, there is no escape from this. We're all going to die."

Rakel held her hand up, palm out. "Ben, you've had a lot to process, you're just panicking. This place is going to blow any second. We need to get out of here now. I promise it'll be okay."

"You promise? I promised Alison I'd save her and now look at her. I can't take it... I just can't!"

"Keep your voice down," Ward demanded.

Ben looked down at Alison, then at Ward. He shrugged, pulled back the hammer on the gun, pointed it to his temple, and began squeezing the trigger.

"No!" Rakel screamed as the gunshot reverberated through the cavern.

Ward looked down the hill and noticed the screamers looking their way, with several heading towards the tunnel entrance.

"Fuck!"

Using his good hand, he grabbed Rakel, moved past Ben's body, and ran back into the tunnel, an awful screeching growing louder and closer behind them. He felt the left wall as he led them along, telling Rakel to leave the torch off in the hope that the creatures wouldn't be able to see in the dark. Then, all his doubts about their plan were confirmed. From deep within the cave network, a rumbling shook the ground and walls and a deafening boom burst up the tunnel, with hot air whooshing past them.

"The Frankies!" Rakel screamed. "There's no way out!"

Ward pulled her to him and held her. Rocks and debris fell from the roof and walls around them. Screeching from behind made him look back, just in time to see the creatures crushed by a mass of crumbling rock and ice, with others crawling forward, determined to get to them. Ahead, the tunnel lit up in a red glow, with an intense heat coming at them.

"The cap is blown," he shouted. "The vent is open!"

More rock fell and tremors split the ground beneath them, opening fissures, with ice-water pouring in above and behind them, steam hissing and billowing everywhere.

"Fuck." He tried his best to remain calm as death shot at them from every angle. There was no way out of it. "I've got you. I've got you."

All for nothing.

Another fissure split in the wall behind them – a dark gap descending into the unknown, belching chunks of ice, rock, and steam towards them.

Then a roar filled the tunnel and they gasped at the sight of a wall of lava thundering their way, sizzling and spitting – destroying everything in its path. It was almost upon them when Rakel broke free from his hold and shoved him away from her. He reached to grab her, only to catch hot air. Then he was weightless, and he realized he was falling into the fissure. The last thing he saw before disappearing into it was Rakel enveloped in the ferocious lava flow, then gravity and darkness took him.

TWENTY-TWO

While he'd given himself over to the inevitability of death, the fall was unexpectedly smooth, almost like free-falling down a vertical slide. It couldn't last long, not with the red glow chasing him down the vent, the boiling heat burning his lungs with each strangled breath. The fissure narrowed and widened as he plummeted deeper and deeper, with constant tremors bouncing him from one side to another, until he was numb from so many hard-hitting impacts to every part of his body.

Then the heat didn't seem so intense anymore, and he thought he'd sped up so much he'd outrun the lava flow. But he still fell, until he didn't, and everything ended.

TWENTY-THREE

He woke to a horrible taste of salt water in his mouth and the sound of the sea somewhere in the distance. His limbs trembled as he struggled onto his knees, and cried out when he put pressure on his wrist wound. *What the...?* He shook water off his face and out of his eyes and took in his surroundings. *I'm in a massive cave? On the bank of a wide pool...* Way above him, a black-rock ceiling, with ice-water dripping around him. *I'm alive! The water and soggy sand must have broken my fall.*

With every part of him aching, he managed to get to his feet, the side of his head pounding from the wound. He patted himself down with his good hand. Nothing seemed to be broken.

He took another look around, then up to the light, where the sound of the sea was coming from. It meant a climb of a hundred metres or so, but at least the way wasn't sheer. He could get over the rocks. A smell caught his attention – something acrid – that had no place by the sea. Burning? Fire? Not really surprising when the whole mountain had exploded. *How long have I been out? Is the lava still flowing? Did the screamers survive?*

For the next hour or so, he made a slow, breathless climb up over rock and ice, slipping and cursing, but always dragging himself back to his feet. When he stood at the jagged mouth of the cavern, it was like a man seeing the world for the first time.

No screamers.

No slime.

He made his way along the rock-strewn beach to his right, hoping to see Vík when he rounded the large mounds, but all he saw were plumes of smoke spiralling into the sky. Red embers floated about, mixing with the sea breeze and misty rain. Then he stopped dead when he spotted the village in the distance, covered in a thick cloud of black smoke.

Fuck. He'd emerged from a split in a cliff, about a half-mile from the village.

As he got closer, hot air burned his lungs. *This is what walking through hell must feel like.* The tarmac on the road, almost melting, stuck to the soles of his shoes, forcing him to move along the coastline.

It seemed to take an age, but when he reached the outskirts of the village, he climbed up from the beach and crossed the scorched and pitted football pitch, shocked at what lay before him.

Vík was burning, with cracks and fissures everywhere. Roads, footpaths and all the grass were scorched black, with spluttering lava streams oozing from random places, the substance setting alight everything it touched. An apocalyptic landscape, like nothing he'd ever seen outside of a disaster film.

He walked along the shattered road, with not a single person to be seen. It really was like hell had been unleashed on Earth. The four horsemen had come, blazed everything in their path, before moving on to their next port of call.

Tears prickled the backs of his eyes, but he wouldn't let them come, even though everything he knew and held close was gone. Through the clouds and smoke, something caught his eye. The church on the hill, untouched and still overlooking everything.

Coughing, wheezing, and constantly stumbling, he made his way through fire and smoke, up the hill towards the red-roofed building, eventually finding himself standing in the car park. He couldn't deny the sense of awe at this sentinel remaining untouched by the fiery monster from below. With hardly any energy left, he sat at the doorway, overwhelmed by everything that had brought him here. He looked down at Vík, the village glowing red and orange – steaming – as if releasing everything bad that had been bubbling for so long beneath it. And that's when the tears came and his vision blurred.

His constant wish for death seemed so far away now, like all his family and friends, gone to a better place, living or dead. His efforts to save his people had failed and all had been lost. But then he sat up as a realisation came: unknown to billions of strangers, the sacrifices made in this remote corner of the world had saved them all. So many were alive because of his efforts.

Even through tears, he had to laugh, spluttering hearty snots as he surveyed the burning village below. He took a deep breath and released it into the future, and with it, the weight of the world lifted from his shoulders... the blackening of Vík, his ultimate salvation.

ACKNOWLEGEMENTS

In no particular order, Philip Fracassi, Tim Lebbon, Tim Waggoner, Michael Griffin, Eamon Ó Cléirigh, Kenneth W. Cain, Boz Mugabe, Lydia Capuano, Brian Smyth, Guðmundur Óli Pálmason, Eyvindur Gauti, Rut Jökulskyndill Andresdóttir, Sadie Hartmann, Adam Nevill, Steve Stred, Ray Palen, Marie McWilliams, Glenn Parker, Janelle Janson, T.E. Grau, Barry Keegan, Trevor Kennedy, Adrian Coombe, Jude Purcell, Kevin McHugh and Orla O'Connor.

ABOUT THE AUTHOR

SEÁN O'CONNOR is an award-nominated author, primarily known for his work in Horror and Dark Fiction. He and his family currently reside in Dublin, Ireland.

ALSO AVAILABLE FROM
CADAVER HOUSE

KEENING COUNTRY

SEÁN O'CONNOR

A collection of experimental fiction ranging from creepy horror to powerful explorations of the human mind... ...In *Aerials*, strange antennas dot the landscape from out of nowhere and a tech worker's sister has been found dead, trusting her into a race against time to discover the truth before lies become fact... ...*Down Below* is a story about a boy who stumbles upon a dark family secret beneath the garden shed. A secret his father would do anything to keep buried... ...*Seven Years Gone* is a creepy tale of loss and suffering in which a train driver struggles to overcome haunting visions of his dearly departed... ...In *The Obsessed*, a young girl is infatuated with the older man next door. However, her dream crush has a lust that she will never be able to quench — unless she acquires a similar appetite...

"Visceral, compelling, *Keening Country* packs a considerable punch. Read it and keep your eyes peeled for O'Connor's next work."

— John Langan
Author of *Children of the Fang
and Other Genealogies*

ALSO AVAILABLE FROM
CADAVER HOUSE

THE SWARM

SEÁN O'CONNOR

A swarm of deadly creatures came one night, forever changing the world in this post-apocalyptic horror, leaving a father and son stranded near the Arctic after their plane crashed. Lost in the wilderness, they must decide whether to remain in the relative safety of their makeshift camp or to embark on a deadly trek into the bitter unknown.

"With echoes of Cormac McCarthy's *The Road*, *The Swarm* is a tension-filled apocalyptic nightmare... as stark and unrelenting and chilling as its Arctic setting."

— **Richard Chizmar**
New York Times best-selling author

ALSO AVAILABLE FROM
CADAVER HOUSE

WEEPING SEASON

SEÁN O'CONNOR

In the spirit of Charlie Brooker's *Black Mirror* and *The Twilight Zone* comes Weeping Season — an unsettling, suspenseful chiller that leaves you gasping for breath...

A group of strangers wake up in a cold isolated forest with no memory of anything before their arrival. Lost, hungry and wandering aimlessly, they are summoned to a campsite by a remote entity who controls their fate through a series of tortuous objectives. Their only hope for survival is either escape from the psychological game reserve, known as Block 18, or face mortality at the hands of its maniacal moderator, who loves nothing more than watch his participants suffer...

"Fast, thrilling, and brutal, Weeping Season leaves you gasping for breath. O'Connor's prose is sharp and lean, and he has a great eye for the grisly. Thoroughly recommended."

— **Tim Lebbon**
New York Times bestselling
author of *The Silence*